Richard Mansfield

Don Juan, a play in four acts by Richard Mansfield

Richard Mansfield

Don Juan, a play in four acts by Richard Mansfield

ISBN/EAN: 9783743356658

Manufactured in Europe, USA, Canada, Australia, Japa

Cover: Foto ©Andreas Hilbeck / pixelio.de

Manufactured and distributed by brebook publishing software (www.brebook.com)

Richard Mansfield

Don Juan, a play in four acts by Richard Mansfield

DON JUAN

A Play
In Four Acts

BY

RICHARD MANSFIELD

NEW-YORK
PUBLISHED FOR THE AUTHOR
BY J. W. BOUTON, 8 WEST 28th STREET
1891

Characters.

Don Juan.

Don Luis.

Don Alonzo.

Guzman.

Leporello.

Sebastien.

Donna Julia.

Donna Emilia.

Donna Elvira.

Lucia.

Geralda.

Zerlina.

Anna.

Attendant.

DON JUAN.

✠

𝔄ct 𝔒ne.

A Room in the House of the Count de Marana.

[*Guzman discovered.*

Guzman.

In truth I am weary of this struggle. Could any life be sadder life than mine? than mine! Preceptor and spy. A creature of the inquisition. And for what? To keep the flesh on these old bones. And yet another who loved not these wards of mine might work them harm, and thus, altho' compelled to duty to the inquisition, I can yet guide and counsel in this family so that it commit no wrong. I am an ambassador to a foreign state, who serves his country and the state accredited. Young Don Juan gives me much cause for fear, that his love of adventure and his reckless courage will lead him to some pitfall, and gazing at the stars see not the abyss yawning at his feet. Yet I was once like this—I, too. My days were spent in dreams, in dreams of ambition and of love, and now they 're dreams indeed—and naught is left but to totter on the path that brings each footstep nearer to the Wonderful. Last night I dreamt that I was young, and stood by the window looking out upon the night. Beneath me lay the churchyard, green and silent in the moon, and sycamores and willows whispered to the dead. I dreamt the phantoms of my past rose from their graves and all that might have been else than toil and care and pain;—she, too, was there, Julia of the raven tresses and the star-bright eyes. She opened her arms and called to me and beckoned, as she had called and beckoned in the long ago, and NOW I went to her, and her arms were about me and her perfumed tresses were upon my face— and I awoke—an old man upon the bed of loneliness and sorrow. A life of drudgery, an old age of regrets, a future of speculation. 'T is my duty to teach my pupil thus, the youthful Don Juan, to make his life what mine has been, in great respect and vast propriety! So thus I speak to him without one jot of pleasure in my task, and he, he looks on me, and in his eyes I read: Old man, thou liest; or another time, Thou enviest me my youth; or again, Wouldst thou be thus if thou wert young? And

I long to cry to him: Live! Live! Live! But hither comes "Lucia," the light of my life, my only joy to-day.

[*Enter Lucia. She carries in her arms and in the folds of her dress a mass of flowers.*

Lucia.

Ah, Guzman! good Guzman, I give you good morning! See, I have brought you some flowers to brighten this dull room; every blossom bears in its bosom a tiny ray of yellow sunlight, and the fragrance of our mother earth, and God's free air. See, I will shower them upon you and give a kiss besides, and that vast frown will disappear and you will smile. For you *can* smile! I saw you smile one day, and I wrote that evening in my book thus, "Guzman smiled." But where is my fair cousin Don Juan? I think— altho' I'm not conceited, mark you, Guzman—he doth stand in need of learning more than I! He is a lay-a-bed. Tell me, good Guzman, did'st thou hear aught last night? I thought I heard Don Juan's voice and the clash of steel. No, not in the street— for there the watchman cried "All's well"—but in the garden. Did you, Guzman, did you?—or did I dream? I do dream so much. Dost ever dream, Guzman? [*Falling back with a sigh.*] No, I suppose not. Tell me, Guzman, will you, why do I always dream of Don Juan?

2

Guzman.

You dream of Don Juan?—you never told me
this !

Lucia.

No?—and yet I know not why I should not. I
dream of him always. Tell me why, Guzman—you
who know everything.

Guzman.

Because, my child, he is your cousin, and you are
much together.

Lucia.

But I am more with you, Guzman, and I do never
dream of you.

Guzman.

Perhaps you like him better than your aged preceptor.

Lucia.

I know not. Do I? I love you very much. I
wonder what I should do without you? I see so little
of Don Juan. Don Luis is so stern, Donna Emilia so severe, the house so gloomy—only you and
my books and the garden—ah, yes, the garden !
Sometimes he sits with me half an hour in the arbor
or lies at my feet on the terrace—but 't is only when
he 's tired—yet I am happy then. Guzman, do you
love Don Juan as much as I do? Does everybody
love him ?

Guzman.

Aye, everybody.

Lucia, with a sigh.

Yes, I thought so—everybody. [*Voices are heard without.*] Guzman, Don Luis comes and Donna Emilia, and if they find not Don Juan at his studies they will surely punish him. Let me escape by the window and find him!

Guzman.

Hasten then, my child, if you would save him.

Lucia.

Yes—oh, yes!

> [*Exit at the window* L. *Enter Don Luis and Donna Emilia. Guzman rises.*

Don Luis.

Guzman, where is your pupil?

Guzman.

Sir, I await him here.

Don Luis.

But here he should be now. Hast sent for him? I think 't is long past the hour; what discipline is this?

Guzman.

Sir, can the old man tame a wild colt?

Don Luis.

Then must I employ those who can. Go, sir, seek him, and know your place depends upon your haste.

[*Guzman bows and exit* R.

Donna Emilia.

The severity of your plans for the education of Don Juan seem, Don Luis, to bear but sorry fruit. I think he pays but little heed to the rules laid down for him.

Don Luis.

Madame, your son —

Donna Emilia.

Our son!

Don Luis.

Very well, if you wish, *our* son—our son may perchance prefer the simple delights of the garden or, weary with the studies of the night,—for I doubt not he burns the midnight oil,—be still a-bed. *My* couch offers but little inducement; with him 't is otherwise —he rests in peace with innocence.

Donna Emilia.

For which reason you seek your rest elsewhere.

Don Luis.

Madame, within these walls we will respect the proprieties. Beneath this roof, which shelters Don Juan, no word must be uttered to stain with a breath the pure innocence of *his* nature. I vow Don Juan shall never hear from me one word against his mother.

Donna Emilia.

And never will I utter aught against the spotless reputation of his father—although, alas! I fear he may learn elsewhere—

Don Luis.

Never, madame; in Sevilla no man is more respected than I. I have at all times taken the greatest pains to ward off scandal.

Donna Emilia.

I, too, have been most careful.

Don Luis.

You are a model wife!

Donna Emilia.

Is there household more honored than ours? The severity of our morals and our manners are the talk of Sevilla. It is esteemed a high favor to be recog-

nized by us; we give largely to the church; when we
ride or walk abroad all bow to us—

Don Luis.

Your aristocratic bearing, Donna Emilia, when
seated in your high carriage, and lifting your eye-
brows—thus—is, I confess, just what it should be;
certainly no one suspects—

Donna Emilia.

Not a soul! It is exceedingly pleasant to be so
much respected.

Don Luis.

We have enjoyed our lives; let us not reproach
ourselves with it.

Donna Emilia.

I have no intention of so doing.

Don Luis.

Still, I might prefer that Don Juan should follow
our example only as far as its appearance, and not its
reality, may be concerned. I am anxious to prove
the result of my training.

Donna Emilia.

He has been educated with the greatest austerity.

Don Luis.

The association with youths of his own age has been denied him; his morals might be corrupted.

Donna Emilia.

With young women he has never spoken, unless it be his cousin Lucia, who has shared his education.

Don Luis.

No books which might enlighten him has he read.

Donna Emilia.

The garden, the park, the innocent pastimes guarded and watched by his aged preceptor.

Don Luis.

His constant association with me—

Donna Emilia.

And with me—

Don Luis and Donna Emilia.

You are sure you have never?

Don Luis.

I have been most guarded.

Donna Emilia.

I have been as innocent as Lucia.

Don Luis.

I have never cursed in his presence.

Donna Emilia.

He has every accomplishment.

Don Luis.

He has every virtue.

Donna Emilia.

The very existence of such a son would refute in the future—

Don Luis.

Any reflection upon our honorable reputation.

[*Loud knocking without. Enter Leporello.*

Don Luis.

What is the noise without, Leporello? Why do you disturb us?

Leporello.

Sir, the noise without is the Duke Alonzo, whose appearance is that of a person in a great rage. I peeped at him through the grille, and his face is very red.

Donna Emilia.

Our neighbor, Don Alonzo? [*Aside.*] What brings him here?—surely he is not rash enough—

Don Luis.

Our dear neighbor, Don Alonzo—[*Aside*] he cannot have discovered my affection for his sister! Shall we see him, Donna Emilia?

Donna Emilia.

I think if you—

Don Luis.

I was about to ask you—   [*Loud knocking.*

Leporello.

Don Alonzo appears to be impatient.

Don Luis.

Well, well, admit him, Leporello, but cautiously — cautiously. Does he appear to be armed?

Leporello.

He is stuck all over with daggers and pistols, and carries a great sword; his face is very red. [*Loud knocks.*] He is also knocking very loudly.

3

Don Luis.

Blockhead, anybody can hear that.

Leporello.

The neighbors are assembling in great throngs — all the windows in the street are open.

Donna Emilia.

Hasten, Leporello, and open the gate. I will leave Don Luis to speak with the Duke alone.

Don Luis.

By no means, madame. Stay, Leporello.

[*Loud knocking.*

Leporello.

Sir, I fear the gate will fall.

Don Luis.

Admit him, and bring my sword, Leporello, and remain within call. Stay—where is your master, Don Juan ?

Leporello.

Don Juan ?

Don Luis.

Yes, idiot, Don Juan.

Leporello.

Oh, Don Juan, sir; he is in the chapel praying.

[*Exit.*

Donna Emilia.

Saintly youth. [*Exit.*

Don Luis.

Would that my conscience were as clear as our son's.

[*Enter the Duke of Navarro furiously. He carries in one hand a sword; the other arm is in a sling.*

Don Alonzo.

Ah, you are there! Like father, like son!

Don Luis.

Good morning, my lord; this is a beautiful compliment you have paid me. But why, my dear neighbor, this anger — this noise?

Don Alonzo.

This anger, this noise, Don Luis? I have been robbed of my wife.

Don Luis.

Happy man!

Don Alonzo.

Sir?

Don Luis.

Unhappy man, I congratulate —

Don Alonzo.

Sir ?

Don Luis.

I sympathize with you; how was this happy — unhappy event —

Don Alonzo.

Enough! Don Luis! I hold you responsible,—my
wife has left me.

Don Luis.

I always warned you that it was a mistake —

Don Alonzo.

Enough! I hold you, Don Luis, responsible for the
conduct of your son.

Don Luis.

Sir, you are dreaming. My son is a saint — even
now he is in the chapel praying.

Don Alonzo.

'T is well that he prays, for his last hour is come;
his blood shall wipe out the stain.

[*Enter Guzman with Lucia by window.*

Don Luis.

Pray, Guzman, speak to the Duke. His Highness is excited and laboring under the strangest delusion. He speaks in the wildest and most incoherent manner.

Guzman.

Pray, my lord, what is troubling you?

Don Alonzo.

Troubling me! Ah, Guzman, I have been robbed of my young wife.

Guzman.

Ah — alas! [*Aside.*] Withdraw, Lucia.

[*Lucia stands still.*

Don Alonzo.

Last night I woke — I was alone. I sprang from my couch — the window opening into the garden was open — I heard voices — in the moonlight I recognized my wife, Donna Julia, in the arms of —

Guzman.

[*Stepping forward hastily.*

Pray, my lord, be silent; I understand —

Lucia. [*Stepping forward.*

Poor Don Alonzo, who has robbed you of your wife?

Don Alonzo.

His example of purity, his saint.

Guzman.

Oh, hush — hush!

Don Alonzo.

Don Juan.

Lucia.

[*Stands with eyes wide open.*

Oh — that hurts — that hurts — I wonder — why —

Guzman.

My poor Lucia, what a rude awakening! Why need she suffer so soon? Come, Lucia, come hence.

Lucia.

Good Guzman, something has broken in my heart.

Don Luis.

Sir, you presume upon your high rank and your power to insult an innocent family.

Don Alonzo.

Listen, and judge if I presume. I attacked your pestilent son; after a few passes his sword pricked my arm, my weapon dropped to the ground, and he escaped. My wife, too, has fled; I have not seen her since.

Don Luis.

You were deceived, sir, by the darkness; my son himself shall tell you of his innocence. Leporello— hey, Leporello!

Guzman.

Come, my child, come away.

Lucia.

No, Don Juan approaches; let me stay. He will say that it is not true. And yet last night I heard—

[*Enter Leporello.*

Leporello.

My master, sir, is coming hither. Poor saint, he was barely able to don his clothes; his back was streaming with blood.

Don Luis.

With blood?

Lucia.   [*Aside.*

Then it *was* he—he was wounded!

Leporello.

Aye, sir. Not content with kneeling for hours upon a stone floor strewn with peas—he bared his shoulders and commanded me to flagellate him.

Don Luis.

Wretch! And you obeyed?

Leporello.

Oh, sir, how could I refuse his saintly behest? Often do my master and I in our religious fervor castigate each other. I begged him to excuse me, but he would not hear me, and so I beat him soundly.

Don Alonzo.

Hypocrite!

Don Luis.

My poor boy.

Leporello.

But here comes my master.

Lucia.

Good Guzman—do not leave me.

[*Enter Don Juan.*

Don Alonzo.

Don Juan, answer me: where is the Duchess de Navarro?

Don Juan.

The Duchess, sir, I hope is where she should be— at early matins. What is this noise, father? Why am I disturbed in my devotions? Lucia—why so pale? and what brings Don Alonzo here so early and so angry?

Don Luis.

Forgive me, my son, but his Highness doth accuse
you of a heinous crime.

Don Juan.

A crime! What is a crime?

Don Alonzo.

Villain!

Don Juan.

Ah!   [*Touches his sword.*

     Don Luis.   [*To Don Alonzo.*

Pray, sir, let me speak, since your mistake carries
your temper with it. Don Juan, my son, forgive me,
I know not how to explain. Don Alonzo is laboring
under the delusion that last night—

Don Juan.

Yes, last night?

Don Luis.

You visited his garden and—spoke with his wife.

Don Juan.

Oh! [*Turning to Don A.*] What made you think,
and why should I desire to speak with your wife?

4

Don Alonzo.

Don Juan, you know well enough. Where is she gone?

Don Juan.

Sir, you are laboring under the strangest delusion; why should I talk to the old lady?

Don Alonzo.

What? You know well that the Duchess is both young and beautiful.

Don Juan.

If that is the case, are you surprised that she should have left you?

Don Alonzo.

This is too much.   [*Advances toward him.*

Don Juan.

Leporello, tie my right arm. I will fight the Duke with my left.

Leporello.

Oh, good master, remember your prayers —[*Whispers*] your father — Donna Lucia.

Don Juan.

Ah, yes, prithee pardon me, my father, pardon me Lucia, but I cannot refuse to meet the Duke; and think ye how kind it will be to set free his young and beautiful wife.

Don Luis.

Enough—enough—nay, put up your sword, my lord. Don Juan, your manner surprises me. Still, it is the indignation of innocence—for you are innocent, my son, are you not?

Don Juan.

I am sorry to say I am.

Don Alonzo.

Ah!

Don Luis.

What?

Don Juan.

What said I?

Don Luis.

You expressed regret for your innocence.

Don Juan.

Aye? Did I? Well, it is so; I am sorry I am innocent.

Don Luis.

What say you?

Don Juan.

Indeed, I would the crime were mine that I might receive the punishment therefor; yet I love the truth too well not to speak it. Poor Leporello!

Don Luis and Don Alonzo.

Leporello?

Leporello.

What!

Don Juan.

I am sorry for you, my poor Leporello, I have warned you so often — I have even thrashed you.

Leporello.

You have, indeed!

Don Juan.

Yet all in vain. Father, poor Leporello — albeit a good servant — hath a great fault. E'en at our devotions 't is easy to see which way his mind doth wander, and whilst you, my father, meant to guard me from all worldly thought of sin, the serpent lay at my very elbow. Fortunate indeed it is I am so buckled in the armor of virtue that no temptation can here penetrate—

but alas! with him no power can persuade, no rigor can restrain, and whilst his hypocrisy is such that he will blind you to the very nature of his mind, the sight of beauty, be she maid or wife, doth so inflame him that his desires rush him on to immediate perdition.

Leporello.

He is describing himself.

Don Juan.

Last night, when overcome with sleep, I dozed upon my knees. He crept away. I awoke to find him gone. My cloak, torn from my back to bare it to the lash—my hat, in reverence thrown upon the flags—my sword, unbuckled lest its clatter stay the current of my thoughts, were taken from my side. The instant thought of danger led me to the gate. I heard the clash of steel, and presently saw I—but no, spare me the recital. Go, Leporello—go—fly, fool! He is upon thee!   [*Exit Leporello.*

Don Luis.

Sir, you thus perceive my son is innocent.

Don Alonzo.

No, sir, I am not thus deceived, and he shall pay me dear for this—

Don Juan.

I 'll meet you, my Lord, when and where you say.

Don Alonzo.

I do not war with boys—I have a surer way.

Don Juan.

Yes, I have heard.

Guzman.

Beware.

Don Luis.

My boy, do not anger his Highness.   My Lord, we are most grieved.

Don Juan.

Nay, we are not—and know, I 'm tired of this cant. Sir, I have lied, and I confess the fault, but I 'm a liar for the cause I 'm taught to lie.   'T was *I* who in the garden sought your wife, yet on my soul by no premeditated deed of hers.   I saw her there and sprang the wall, and, conquered by her beauty, woo'd her on the spot.   She spurned me, I confess—and if she fled, she fled but from your wrath, and usage too, I hear, not over fair.   And now, sir, though you scorn to meet a boy, I 'll fight you like a man, and 't shall go hard, but I will give you much to do.

Don Luis.

My son!

Don Alonzo.

'T is well! I will consider your punishment. Sirs, good day. [*Exit with pages.*

Don Luis.

We are lost.

Don Juan.

Coward!

Guzman.

Don Juan, you have made a bitter enemy.

Lucia. [*Sinks onto seat.*

Don Juan! Don Juan!

Don Juan.

Nay, fair cousin, fear not.

Lucia.

He has a wicked, settled look.

Don Juan.

Some dogs that look the fiercest bite the least.

Guzman.

Not so with Navarro.

Don Luis.

Alas, alas for his day's work! Come, Guzman, go with me. We will wait upon the Duke, and try to turn his wrath.

Don Juan.

Father, I pray you no.

Don Luis.

Boy, when you are older you will know the worth of peace.

Guzman.

Sir, I will go with you, but much I fear it will be all in vain.

Don Luis.

Boy, you will stay here till we return! Come, Guzman.   [*Exit.*

Guzman.   [*To Lucia.*

I leave you with him. Remember, my Lucia, that you may save him by pure and constant love.

Lucia.

Can love and fortitude prevail, I'll never desist.

Guzman.

Farewell. Don Juan, I pray you, listen to your cousin.   [*Exit.*

Don Juan.

Aye, that I will with pleasure! From lips like thine, my sweet Lucia, counsel is honey, and I 'll lie at thy feet and thou shalt preach to me. [*Sits at her feet.*] Lucia, how solemn thou dost look; thou deem'st me very bad, but men are all like this—we hate an ugly face. How could I love thee, Lucia, wert thou not beautiful?

Lucia.

Then thou dost love me?

Don Juan.

Of course I do.

Lucia.

But thou lovest the Donna Julia?

Don Juan.

Not much — she 's very pretty.

Lucia.

Thou canst not love us both?

Don Juan.

Oh, yes.

5

Lucia.

How can that be?

Don Juan.

Oh, I can love a dozen.

Lucia.

That is not love!

Don Juan.

Is it not?   It seemeth to me much like it.

Lucia.

Not true love.

Don Juan.

Aye, but it must be.   Now when I sit at thy feet,
and gaze into thine eyes, and look upon thy coral lips
and thy silken tresses, I have a strange longing—

Lucia.

Yes?

Don Juan.

To kiss thee.

Lucia.

That shalt thou not.

Don Juan.

Ah—

Lucia.

Why dost thou sigh?

Don Juan.

Because when thou sayest I must not, the desire is a thousand times more burning than before. That must be love?

Lucia.

My heart says no. Listen, Don Juan.

Don Juan.

I listen.

Lucia.

I do love thee.

Don Juan.

Then thou wilt kiss me?

Lucia.

Nay, that will I never. I do love thee with all my heart and soul, and I would die for thee if it could serve thee aught, but I will kiss thee, no. Yet thy professions put I to the proof. Thou sayest thou dost love me?

Don Juan.

Aye, come with me, Lucia, let us go, and in some lovely spot we'll dwell and forget aught else but you and I and Love.

Lucia.

That may not be.   Listen.   Thou sayest thou lovest me?

Don Juan.

Aye, I do love thee, Lucia.

Lucia.

Then hear the terms on which I 'll be thy bride.

Don Juan.

My bride?

Lucia.

Didst thou not ask me?   See here this cross, the holiest of symbols, an oath thou darest not break. Wilt swear upon it thus—wilt swear, I say?

> *My bride art thou, Lucia,*
> *Thou my bride,*
> *And I will cleave to thee*
> *Through happiness and sorrow,*
> *Through youth and age,*
> *From here unto the grave.*
> *In word and thought,*
> *In wish and deed,*
> *I will be true to thee,*
> *To thee, Lucia.*

Wilt thou swear thus, and, having sworn, incur the
penalty shouldst fail?   E'en such an oath take I —

Don Juan.

Nay, that were slavery!   [*Springing up.*

Lucia.

Nay, that were love.

Don Juan.

I cannot swear.

Lucia.

Farewell.

Don Juan.

Nay, hold!

Lucia.

Farewell.   That thou dost love me not kills not *my*
love, and I shall pray for strength to guard thee all I
may.   Farewell.

Don Juan.

Alas, farewell; thou art much too good.
                [*Enter Don Luis and Donna Emilia.*

Donna Emilia and Don Luis.

Don Juan!

Don Juan.

You almost frightened me.

Donna Emilia.

Don Juan! We trust we find you in a mood repentant!

Don Juan.

I am very much wearied.

Don Luis.

And we are anxious to learn how one so reared could have behaved as you have done?

Donna Emilia.

And having been bred in ignorance of the very word "love," you entertained such wicked thoughts? You certainly do not take after me!

Don Luis.

Nor, zounds, me!

Don Juan.

It must be one of you!

Don Luis.

Be seated, Donna Emilia, and you, Don Juan, have my permission to be seated. It is necessary we should confer, and having consulted Guzman, your preceptor, now point the wisest way to avert the danger which threatens you, and plan some mode to discipline your

conduct in the future. But first, what explanation—
what excuses can you offer?

Don Juan.

Sir, an had you taught me more, I should have less
inquired; had you less forbidden, I should have less
desired; and had you less temptations shown, I should
have less temptations known.

Donna Emilia.

The sooner the boy leaves the house the better.

Don Luis.

I quite agree with you, and for his own safety's sake
he must be gone at once; nor must the Duke know
whither.

Don Juan.

Whither?

Don Luis.

I know not whither; that is for afterthought. Guzman has pointed a way whereby he thinks the Duke's
wrath may be averted in giving certain surety of Don
Juan's good conduct in the future, and that the Duke's
pleasant domesticity be no further molested. Guzman
suggests a marriage.

Donna Emilia.

That is indeed a certain guarantee.

Don Luis.

There is no difficulty in finding a bride for Don Juan.   Lucia, our ward, is handy.

Don Juan.

Nay, sir, both she and I have something here to say.

Donna Emilia.

What!

Don Juan.

Whether we will or no?

Don Luis.

What 's this?   Your mother ne'er was asked.

Donna Emilia.

Indeed I was not.

Don Luis.

Nor was my sanction sought.   Our parents settled this, and now we settle too.   You wed at once Lucia, our ward; you leave upon a trip; I hasten to the Duke and tell him all is well.   All 's hushed, all 's calm, the house stands, and we and you are saved.

Don Juan.

If Lucia wills, I will; she is a gentle child, and I am fond of her; but if she won't, I won't, nor will I have her inclination forced.

Donna Emilia.

Tut, tut, what tone is this? Here comes Lucia, and we will swiftly acquaint her with our purpose.

Don Luis.

Lucia. Ahem!

Don Juan.

Ahem!

Lucia.

Pray, sir, what is it?

Donna Emilia.

There is no need to make the story long. Lucia, you are to wed Don Juan, our son.

Lucia.

Oh!

Don Juan.

Fair, sweet Lucia, if you will.
6

Don Luis.

If you will — 't is all the better; if you will not —
't is all the same — you must.

Lucia.

Forgive me, Don Juan, I will not, for you do not
love me.

Don Juan.

I am not sure.

Lucia.

Therefore, I will not.

Donna Emilia.

Love has nothing to do with it — eh, Don Luis?

Don Luis.

Nothing, I vow; it 's a mere case of convenience.

Lucia.

Sir, I regard it higher, and I cannot.

Donna Emilia.

Then you must. You are our ward, on us entirely
dependent. Refuse, and you are roofless, penniless,
outcast.

Don Luis.

It 's hard, but so it is.

Don Juan.

'T is infamous; she shall not be so forced.

Lucia.

Nor can I be. I love thee, Don Juan, and I have told thee so, but till thou knowest thyself I cannot give myself to thee.

Don Juan.

'T is true, I do not know — and yet I would protect thee.

Lucia.

Nay, dear cousin, we shall meet again, and then perchance thou 'lt love me.

Don Juan.

I think I love thee now.

Lucia.

But thou knowest not?

Don Juan.

No, I know not.   [*Enter Guzman.*

Don Luis.

What flummery is this! Hey, Guzman, here, and
teach your pupils more obedience. They are to wed
—'t is needed; we will it so, and they refuse.

Guzman.

You refuse, Don Juan?

Don Juan.

For she declines, since I know not if I love her.

Guzman.

You decline?

Lucia.

Yes.

Don Luis.

Then hear me well. Thou art outcast, Lucia, outcast from our house. Take what you need — begone;
we've nursed you, sheltered you, and for reward such
base ingratitude! Begone! Love — pah — what is love
compared with honor, safety, and position!

Lucia.

Sir, I obey. Madame,— sir, farewell. I thank you
from my heart for all your kindness, all your care. I
should despise myself if, for the comfort of my body,

I sacrificed my soul. Don Juan, pray think of me sometimes — farewell. [*Exeunt Guzman and Lucia.*

Don Juan.

Sweet cousin, we shall meet again, I trow, and soon.
[*Enter Leporello.*

Leporello.

Oh, master, Donna Elvira comes, and will hear no denial.

Don Juan. [*Aside.*

Lead her the other way.

.

Leporello.

Nay, sir, she knows you 're here.

Don Luis.

Of whom speak you, knave? Donna Elvira, sister to the Duke?

Don Juan.

Aye, sir; doubtless to pay her respects to you, and by your lief once I 'm to go, I 'll lose no time, but instantly be gone.

Don Luis.

Stay. Perchance the lady brings important message from the Duke.

Don Juan.

I 'll meet her and inquire.

Don Luis.

Stay!

Don Juan. [*Aside.*

Go, Leporello, intercept her; say I will meet her in the garden at the proper hour.

Leporello.

I fly, sir.

Don Luis.

Stay!

Leporello.

I stay, sir. [*Aside.*] You see I cannot fly.

Don Juan.

Fool, you should have acted sooner.

[*Enter Donna Elvira.*

Donna Elvira.

Ah, you are here. I 'm glad to find you all. Ah, Don Juan, I came to warn you. Sir,—madame, your obedient servant. [*Courtesies.*] There is no need for more concealment, naughty boy. The sooner now 't is known the better. I 'd a mind to make a confidant of the Duke. Naughty boy, naughty boy. I am not angry with thee.

Don Luis and Donna Emilia.

Oh, madame, you are most good, and you will intercede with his Highness for this wayward youth?

Donna Elvira.

I know not yet — first I will hear his excuses.

Don Juan.

Pray, madame, come and take a walk.

Donna Elvira.

Not yet — not yet. Who 'd have thought thee so inconstant?

Don Juan.

Pray, madame, take a walk.

Donna Elvira.

Presently, dear Don Juan, your good parents must know all.

Don Juan.

They know enough already.

Donna Emilia.

Alas! madame, we know all.

Donna Elvira.

And has he told you already? Reckless boy!

Don Juan.

Yes, yes, the whole story is told.

Donna Emilia.

Alas! madame, we know everything. Was ever tale so sad?

Don Luis.

We feel our disgrace, madame.

Donna Elvira.

Disgrace, sir? What! disgrace! Call you it disgrace for your son to win the hand of Donna Elvira de Navarro?

Don Juan.

Zounds, madame, I thought you were more coy.

Donna Elvira.

Tush, tush, dear Don Juan—now you are so bitterly attacked, accused, wronged, endangered, and reviled, who should stand by you if not I—your bride?

Don Luis.

Madame, this is most sudden.

Donna Emilia.

This is a great honor, and, Don Juan, it makes noble amends for your slight flirting.

Donna Elvira.

I forgive that—he has loved me long. Is it not so, Don Juan?

Don Juan. [*Looking at her.*

Yes, 't is an old love.

Don Luis.

Don Juan seems to have spent much time in our neighbor's house?

Donna Elvira.

Poor loving boy, he could not keep away. Come, good people, give us your blessing.

Don Luis.

That will I gladly.

Donna Emilia.

And I.

Don Juan.

Stay. No, Donna Elvira. I cannot accept this noble sacrifice. I cannot, and I will not. I am unworthy of thee—unworthy of thy noble virtues and thy beauty. I am overcome with the knowledge of my guilt, and I must expiate my crime. I here renounce all pretensions to that fair hand—I am not worthy or it. Heaven knows the nature of the sacrifice, how great it is! Farewell, Donna Elvira. Farewell, father; farewell, mother. Come, Leporello, you

7

shall share my exile. Donna Elvira, forgive, forget,
a wretched youth who loves you so that he would
rather leave you than pollute your love. Farewell.

[*Exit weeping.*

Leporello.

Farewell.   [*Exit weeping.*
                    [*Donna Elvira sinks fainting.*

[CURTAIN.]

Act Two.

Act Two.

✠

Don Juan.

This hostelry will do as well, for want of a better.

Leporello.

Nay, methinks 't is very well indeed, master, and my bones ache for jolting of that mule.

Don Juan.

I 'll warrant the mule aches for jolting of thee, donkey.

Leporello.

A feather bed is better than the damp grass whereon we lay last night!

Don Juan.

I slept well enough, albeit a dream, which I have a mind to tell thee.

Leporello.

Rum tum tum, rum tum tum.

Don Juan.

'Sdeath, I 'll rum tum tum thy pate. What is this?

Leporello.

Pardon, master, but I do never hear one say he will tell of a dream but I bethink me of the player who steppeth to the lamps thus, and saith: List and I'll tell thee my dream of last night—Rum tum tum, rum tum tum.

Don Juan.

Cease thy prattle, and listen to my dream, which I pour into thee for lack of a better receptacle.

Leporello.

If you would pour a dram into me, master, it would be a dream indeed, and I know of a dream of a dram I have dreamt of.

Don Juan.

Thou shalt have the dram after the dream, but if thou cease not gabbling, it shall be a drumming and no dramming I'll give thee.

Leporello.

Zounds, sir, I am speechless.

Don Juan.

I am not given much to serious dreaming, but thus I dreamt last night. Back was I in Sevilla. I recognized my own gloomy chamber in which I paced, and fretted as I paced. I seemed to be burning with desire of the world, and a great longing and striving for the blue sky, and the sun, and the green trees, and the scent of sweet flowers; my mind ran full of grassy slopes and shady arbors, of fair faces and glistening shapes, of sparkling cups, of tinkling music, of perfumes and rich dresses. But the door was bolted, the windows barred. And as I paced as a lion in a cage, I knew a strength within me to burst the very walls of stone. Youth coursed through my veins like molten fire, my voice rang to the heavens and I would have soared aloft with it. Is there a power, quoth I, to rid me of thraldom? Is there a power, quoth I, to give me all youth's desires: love, wealth and freedom, and strength and health and power? As I spake there came a knocking and the bar fell from the door, and there entered one shaped and dressed as a man, yet in all else different though I knew not wherein it lay. "I come," said he, "at your bidding." To which I answered: "I know you not." "Nay," quoth he, "in truth thou hast never met me, yet I am an old friend of thy father's, and he has had many dealings with me. I am willing to serve his son, and can accomplish for thee all thy desires. Thou shalt have all the earth affords of pleasure.

Leporello.

I tremble, master. How was this man dressed?— was he not all in red, with a high-peaked cap and a tall feather, mustachios pointed toward the eyes and a goat's beard?

Don Juan.

Nay, he was most soberly clad in black, and had a scholarly appearance.

Leporello.

The saints be praised! I feared it was the devil.

Don Juan.

'T was he. But mind, 't is only a dream. The devil was a most agreeable person, affable and hearty, with a wonderful power of conversation and entertainment. We soon closed a bargain.

Leporello.

A bargain with the devil! Master, I must leave you.

Don Juan.

Stay, fool, 't is only a dream.

Leporello.

I like not such dreams.

Don Juan.

I was to be furnished health, wealth, love from all, pleasures unbounded, and, in return, when I died the devil would call for me.

Leporello.

Master! Master!

Don Juan.

Now I bethink me, there was a saving clause.

Leporello.

Master, master! I warrant 't is a hard one.

Don Juan.

Ay. Should one pure woman love me and still withstand *me* and the power of the devil, then—even at the last hour—he could not claim me. But 't was all a dream—and, Leporello, I 'm young—I 'm happy —I 'm free—I 'll love—I 'll enjoy this beautiful world, and for the rest—

Leporello.

You 'll go to the devil.

Don Juan.

Who is it comes here?

Leporello.

Mine host of the inn, sir; doubtless to pay his respects. [*To the host, who approaches.*] This, sir, is Don Juan de Marana, a noble gentleman of Sevilla. I am his faithful and valued valet.

8

Host.

Noble sir, you are most welcome to my house. My servants bring a cup of welcome. 'T is a noble wine, sir, and grown on the hills here.

[*Servants approach with wine.*

Don Juan.

My pleasures begin—give me the cup. [*Drinks.*] And now, sir, your wine is good—what pleasures doth your town afford?

Host.

Sir, we have theatres.

Don Juan.

Theatres! I have been to them, eh, Leporello? At night, eh? In capital disguises we went. Pray, what plays play you, and what theatres have you? This seems a small place?

Host.

Sir, we have fifteen theatres and some eight odd cheaper places of resort.

Don Juan.

Zounds, man! and what's your population?

Host.

Some fifteen thousand, and growing.

Don Juan.

A thousand to a theatre; well, and the plays?

Host.

"The Conspirators," for tragedy.

Don Juan.

We saw that in Sevilla.

Host.

"The Blind Girl of Saragossa," for drama.

Don Juan.

We saw that too.

Host.

"The Calumny," for high comedy.

Don Juan.

We saw that often.

Host.

"The Jockey's Revenge," for melodrama.

Don Juan.

Zounds, man! give us something new!

Host.

"The Weather Vane" — 't is a farce — "The Spider and the Web," "The Actor's Ransom," the burlesque of "Perfidio," and the opera of "Radamisto."

Don Juan.

Why, man, we 've seen them all. Do you nothing new here?

Host.

Oh, no, master, the people would not permit it. We import everything, and we like foreign actors best.

Don Juan.

Then I 'll to no theater. What else is stirring?

Host.

Much scandal, little truth, and some conjecture.

Don Juan.

What is the scandal?

Host.

Sir, the town 's full of it. I know some two dozen scandals, but, by your leave, I am somewhat pressed to-day, as for a truth — I 'm to be married.

Don Juan.

To be married! Why, man, thou art upon sixty if a day?

Host.

Certes, good sir, sixty-five.

Don Juan.

And your bride?

Host.

Close on twenty.

Don Juan.

An' she marries you for love?

Host.

Sir, in our town none but fools marry for love; the women wed for support, the men for convenience.

Don Juan.

And you wed to-day?

Host.

Within the hour the beautiful Zerlina, and if not too bold, I beg the honor of your presence at the ceremony and in the dance on the green this evening.

Don Juan.

Zounds, man! with pleasure. [*Exit host. Anna appears.*] And odds I 'll add another scandal to thy list. Zounds! Leporello, have the flowers come to life, and is yon blossom walking hither?

Leporello.

He 's drunk! How I envy him.

Don Juan.

Surely, 't is a fairy bower this, where such dainty lilies wander?

Leporello.

Oh, heavenly drunk!

Don Juan.

Leporello, see you yonder maiden, how airily she walks, what pert and pretty air she hath, and how her hair shimmers in the sunlight?

Leporello.

Sir, I see a stiff little girl, neither child nor woman, and reeking, no doubt, of pap and porridge.

Don Juan.

I see a rose-bud; go speak with her and bring her hither.

Leporello.

Pray, sir, what shall I say?

Don Juan.

Say we are troubadours in search of charity.

Leporello.

But, sir, I do not choose to lie.

Don Juan.

Go to! Every good servant must be a good liar. Twang thy guitar to call her notice to us.

Leporello.

What! twang my guitar to a peasant girl?

Don Juan.

Odds fish! fool, why not, if she 's pretty?

Leporello.

Sir, I wager her hands are black.

          [Enter Lucia, disguised as a page.

Don Juan.

I 'll warrant they 're washed in milk.   Give *me* the
guitar.

Leporello.

Sir, some one approaches.

          [Lucia comes down.   Anna draws back.

Don Juan.

Ho! what little master have we here?

Leporello.

Sir, he has a most ferocious appearance.

Don Juan.

He hath a gloomy look, 't is true.

Lucia.   [*Speaking to herself.*

They say that he came hither. How shall I dare accost him? [*Perceiving Don Juan and Leporello.*] Oh, sirs!

Don Juan.

Your servant, sir.

Lucia.

Pray, sir, can you tell me where I may find one Don Juan?

Don Juan.

And what would you with him?

Lucia.

Sir, I seek service with him as a page.

Don Juan.

I think I read this page. You must apply to *this* gentleman.

Lucia.

Sir, but I seek Don Juan.

Don Juan.

'T is he. This is Don Juan, and I am his faithful and valued valet, Leporello.

Lucia.

Sir, by appearances, I should judge you to be Don Juan.

Don Juan.

Youth, you have seen little of the world not to know that the servant is better clad than the master. This gentleman is Don Juan. Sir—are you not Don Juan, sir?

Leporello.

Alas, yes! I am that villain.

Don Juan.

What! And I am his rascally servant, Leporello.

Leporello.

What!

Don Juan.

Sir, I confess I 'm a rascal. I steal your best clothes, your trinkets, and your small change. I live upon you. I drink your wines and I eat your meat, and among my brethren I abuse and malign you. I am a much finer gentleman than you, and 't is only by stress of circumstances I occupy a humble position, for which my accomplishments and my amiable virtues totally unfit me. Pray, sir, accept the service of this honorable youth, and afford me the opportunity of taking my ease even more than I do at present.

Leporello.

You malign yourself, Leporello. I know you to be

9

a noble-minded, honest, virtuous, devoted, long-suffering and abused creature, who will meet his reward only in a better world. But I, your master, am a cross-grained, worthless wretch. I indulge myself in every vice and luxury, careless of the consequences. I regard women as mere slaves to my wishes, and ill-treat and abuse all about me, and I fear to engage the services of this youth lest I return him to his parents contaminated with the atmosphere of my vices.

Don Juan.

A truce. Thou hast so long practised thy art of abuse that I am no match for thee. Certes, youth, I am Don Juan, and take thee into my service if but to prove to thee that I am as innocent and as frolicsome as a lamb.

Lucia.

Sir, I am sure I believe you.

Don Juan.

I will at once initiate thee. Thou knowest the duties of a page?

Lucia.

Sir, to serve you.

Don Juan.

In my pastimes. In all other matters thou art free. I have a mind for love and folly now, since I have led a youth of wisdom, and thou shalt aid me. But since I'm little learned in such matters yet, and thou hast all appearance of a cunning eye and ready tongue—

Lucia.

Nay, nay, sir, I know naught of such matters.

Don Juan.

We'll put it to the proof anon. Here comes a lady.
                              [*Enter Donna Julia.*

Leporello.

Sir, 't is the Donna Julia.

Lucia.

The Donna Julia!   [*Donna Julia comes down.*

Donna Julia.

Don Juan, I know not whether to thank Fortune that I find you or to curse her; it is perchance another evil turn of Fortune's wheel.

Don Juan.

If to cast a humble servant in your way be ill fortune, then Fortune serves you ill. Pray, Donna Julia why alone and sad?

Donna Julia.

Don Juan, I have fled the house of Don Alonzo.

Don Juan.

I do not blame you, madame.

Donna Julia.

There is near here a retreat, a cloister, built upon my land, and yonder now I wend my way, to seek the peace and comfort of its walls. I rest but here a moment on my journey.

Don Juan.

Nay, madame, I will not have it so. You cannot think to hide such beauty from the world.

Donna Julia.

What joys are there for me, wedded to Don Alonzo? But I must not tarry—he follows close, and I endanger you by speaking with you here.

Don Juan.

Pray, Leporello, go and watch by yonder copse and warn if any one approaches. Here, sir — but pray, what's your name?

Lucia.

My name? My name is Guido.

Don Juan.

Well, then, good Guido, you shall add your prayers to mine to keep the Lady Julia here.

Donna Julia.

Sir, do you not perceive that if Don Alonzo discover you with me, an innocent offense will seem a horrid crime. He bears you no good will and would have cause to punish you with instant death.

Lucia.

Aye, Don Juan, pray let the Donna Julia hence.

Don Juan.

What, Guido, is it thus you serve me? Do you not perceive that I adore Donna Julia and would even risk my life for her?

Donna Julia.

Oh, hush! oh, hush! Your love, if love it is, is unrequited.

Don Juan.

Nay, an' for that it burns the fiercer. Think of some argument, think of some spell, good Guido, to bind the Lady Julia here. I cannot bear to have her go.

Lucia.

Sir, sir,—do you love her then so much?

Don Juan.

Canst thou not see how my heart is wrung? Speak to her, beg her to stay.

Lucia.

I cannot.

Don Juan.

Oh, Donna Julia, stay—or better, let us go hence together. Guido, implore her.

Lucia.

I cannot.

Don Juan.

What, Donna Julia, what, Guido, would you see me die of love? Never was Tantalus tormented as am I. What were the fruits that swung above his head, the limpid stream that gurgled at his feet, hunger that could not eat or thirst that could not drink, to unrequited love? Speak for me, Guido.

Lucia.

Pray, madame, go at once.

Don Juan.

What!

Lucia.

Hasten from hence and let your feet have wings.
For every moment 's fraught with danger.

Don Juan.

This is not pleading for me!

Lucia.

He does not love you. It is mere pretense, and
every pretty face can win his fancy.

Don Juan.

You shall leave my service on the spot.

Donna Julia.

Young sir, I do not know you, but you counsel well.

Lucia.

Aye, madame, for I speak the truth. I know a
maiden whom he vowed he loved, and left for that he
knew not if he loved her well enough to wed her.

Don Juan.

Ho! This is treachery!   [*Leporello comes down.*

Leporello.   [*On terrace.*

Sir, sir, the Don Alonzo comes with some ten thousand men!

Don Juan.

Ten thousand!

Leporello.

Or something nigh to that.

Lucia.

Oh, fly, fly.   Donna Julia, go — Oh, Don Juan, now
you are surely lost.

Don Juan.

Come, Donna Julia, let us go.

Lucia.

Stay, sir, I will go with her.

Don Juan.

Thou!   Thou art no protection.

Lucia.

I have a sword.

Don Juan.

Thou hast a toothpick.

Leporello.

Oh, sir, sir, they come.

Lucia.

Don Juan, fly!

Don Juan.

Come, Donna Julia.

Lucia.

Stay !

Don Juan.

First fly, then stay —

Donna Julia.

Farewell, Don Juan.

Don Juan.

Nay, I go too.

Lucia.

And I.

Don Juan.

We do not need thee.

Lucia. [*Stamping foot.*

But I will go !

Don Juan.

Here 's a fine page.

Leporello.

And here he comes.

[*Guzman comes down. Leporello on terrace
rushes at him.*

Leporello.

Down with the villain. Would you dare to attack
my master ? Put up your sword, Sir Duke, or I will
kill you.

10

Guzman.

Fool, what 's this?

Leporello.

Oh, pardon, sir — I thought you were the Duke
come to kill my master, and I was about to destroy
you.

Guzman.

Stand aside, Leporello.

Leporello.

'T is fortunate I stayed my hand.

Guzman.   [*Coming down.*

Donna Julia! How came you here with Don Juan?
I am loath to believe —

Donna Julia.

We met by chance.

Guzman.

Is it truly so?

Lucia.

Yes! Yes!

Guzman.

Whither are you bound, Donna Julia?

Donna Julia.

E'en to my Abbey of the White Ladies.

Guzman.

Madame, by your leave, I will accompany you.

[*Enter above Don Alonzo.*

Don Juan.

Nay, Sir Guzman, I will escort the Lady Julia and protect her.

Don Alonzo. [*On terrace.*

Pardon me, *I* will protect her.

Lucia. [R.

Don Alonzo! Lost!

Don Alonzo.

Madame, pray come here. Sir, you will offer me some explanation for your presence here with the Duchess of Navarro.

Don Juan.

I decline an explanation.

Guzman.

My lord, it is by chance they met. Don Juan being on his travels, the Duchess on the way to her Abbey of the White Ladies.

Don Alonzo.

I do not believe it.

Don Juan.

And I say that Guzman speaks the truth.

Don Alonzo.

And I say that you lie.

Don Juan.

[*Tearing off his glove, throwing it in the face of Don Alonzo.*

This is too much! Now, sir, if you 're a man, or any part or parcel of a man — or the mere semblance or the shadow of a man — you 'll fight.

Don Alonzo.

Guzman, hand me that glove. I accept your challenge, and will send you a messenger anon. And mark me well, Don Juan, this glove shall gag you.

Don Juan.

Sir, if you prove your bragging, you may prove you 're gagging. Pray, let me hear from you without delay.

Don Alonzo.

I 'll wager you will hear from me too soon to please you. Guzman, beware how you anger me. I commit the Donna Julia to your charge. You will at once escort her to the Abbey, where I shall presently join you.   [*Exit Don Alonzo.*

Donna Julia.

Farewell, Don Juan. I implore you not to delay, to place yourself in safety.

Guzman.

Don Juan, I have sad forebodings for your future.

Don Juan.

Nay, sir, I was not born to die so soon.

Guzman.

The morning does not tell the story of the day.

Don Juan.

Go, raven, thou art always croaking. Madame, farewell, for a while. Guzman, be not too harsh with me. I have enjoyed so little yet.

Guzman.

Go to! Go to! Where the sweetest blossoms blow, the deadliest serpents dwell. May heaven guard thee ever and farewell. [*Goes up steps with Donna Julia. Exeunt Donna Julia and Guzman.*

Don Juan.

There, now the clouds are past and, my fair Guido, we may enjoy our lives.

Guido. [L. C.

It seems to me the horizon is very dark.

Don Juan.

Another word like that and I will run thee thro'.
I saw a maiden yonder in the trees—aye, there she
goes. [*Anna comes out* R.

Don Juan.

Now thou shalt help me better than thou didst
awhile ago. Whene'er I 'm short of metaphor, thou
shalt supply the want. Leporello, twang thy guitar.

[*Leporello touches guitar. Anna comes out
under the trees.*

Don Juan.

[*Approaching Anna.*
Pray, tell me, is there only one flower blooming in
all this garden here?

Anna.

Sir, there are flowers all about.

Don Juan. .

I saw but one, but one —

Lucia. [*Prompting him.*
Dandelion.

Don Juan.

Nay, but one rose-bud, and I would pluck it and—

Lucia. [*Prompting him.*

Let it wither.

Don Juan.

Let it wither — nay, wear it near my heart.

Anna. [R.

Sir, I do not understand you.

Don Juan. [R. C.

You do not understand me? Does not your heart tell you that I — I am —

Lucia. [C.

Fooling thee.

Don Juan.

Fooling thee — nay, that I am irresistibly drawn toward thee. When I saw you standing like a —

Lucia.

Gawk.

Don Juan.

Gawk, nay, nay, like a fairy, plucking with those hands so white and —

Lucia.

Bony.

Don Juan.

Bony, nay, nay, slender, the blossoms, I knew I had found at last a little maiden whom I could love and —

Lucia.

Leave.

Don Juan.

No, wed, wed [*Looking at Lucia*], wed! Let us wander — let me tell you a thousand —

Lucia.

Lies.

Don Juan.

Lies! Oh —

> [*Don Juan stamps his foot in anger, and exits hastily with Anna.*

Leporello. [*Seated on bench.*

Rum tum tum. For a thoroughgoing villain, commend me to my master. I 've a mind to trounce him! There 's wine in this stoup still. [*Drinks.*

> [*Enter Sebastien. He is very pale and poorly clad, after the manner of a student.*

Sebastien.

Pray, sir, can you tell me is there a wedding here to-day?

Leporello.

I know for no surety of a wedding, but there are many chances for some funerals.

Sebastien.

True, most true! I know of nothing truer of myself than that.

Leporello.

Sir, are you dying?

Sebastien.

A like to.

Leporello.

Sir, I prithee sit down.   And what is your disease?

Sebastien.

It is of the heart.

Leporello.

Sir, drink of this wine; it will go straight to it.

[*Offers wine.*

Sebastien.

I thank you, sir.   I desire naught to keep life in me.
Did you say the wedding is for to-day?

Leporello.   [*Seated.*

I did hear of a wedding.

Sebastien.

One Zerlina to the aged host of this inn?

Leporello.

Even so.

Sebastien.

Sir, this Zerlina was to be my bride.

Leporello.

And did she flout you?

11

Sebastien.

Nay, she was forced to it.   I am an actor.

Leporello.

[*Moves hastily to the other end of the bench.*
Heaven defend us !

Sebastien.

Sir, I have never done any harm.

Leporello.

I am willing to believe you.   Still, you are ill
spoken of.

Sebastien.

'T is the cause of all my sorrow.   Whilst I amused,
I was tolerated, and mistook toleration for friendship.
When I woo'd the daughter of the house, they mocked
me and thrust me from the door.

Leporello.

You must confess you had much assurance.

Sebastien.

Sir, I am a well-born, well-bred, well-mannered
man, and her father is a tallow-chandler.   They wed
her to an aged liquor-dealer.

Leporello.

Sir, you know the power of gold?

Sebastien.

Sir, I have felt naught but its sting.

Leporello.

Your story, sir, touches me. Can I do aught to help you? [*Enter Don Luis.*] Zounds! an' if that be not Don Luis, write me down ass. Come aside, sir, with me swiftly, and I will tell you what I may do.

Sebastien.

Sir, you are very good.

[*Both exit. Don Luis comes down.*

Don Luis.

The conduct of this boy will bring ruin on our family. It seems that Don Juan came in this direction, and I have ridden hard. [*Attendants commence lighting lamps in garden.*] Ho, man, what is in preparation here?

Attendant.

Sir, the wedding guests will dance on the green anon, and I have orders, by your leave, to light the lamps.

Don Luis.

Whose wedding?

Attendant.

The host of this inn to Zerlina—the belle of the town.

Don Luis.

'T is well.   Weddings, elopements, betrothals! There was a time when I too—what ho—who's this?

                       [*Sebastien approaches.*

Sébastien.

Noble sir, I throw myself upon your mercy.

Don Luis.

Sir, how can I be of service to you?

Sebastien.

Sir, I am a poor student, but of noble birth.

Don Luis.

Speak on.

Sebastien.

In brief, the host of this inn, a man—saving your presence—of great age, by the power of gold and influence has robbed me of my bride. I am assured, sir, that you are a man of unequaled generosity. There is to be a dance here anon. Sir, will you win me back my bride and earn the eternal blessings of a suffering youth?

Don Luis.

I see no way to aid you, if I would.

Sebastien.

[*Turns for approval to Leporello, who stands
behind a tree and nods or shakes his head.*

A gentleman of high rank, who knows you well,
but who saith he hath affairs of his own that hold his
time, hath sent me to you with this message.

Don Luis.

Pray, sir, was it Don Alonzo?

Sebastien.

He bade me not to say.

Don Luis.

Sir, you come well recommended; and since I owe
your friend a heavy debt, I 'll pay it.   Command me.

Sebastien.

Then, sir, the way is this.   You are to elope with
Zerlina after the dance.   The power of your name
and of your friend's — for he doth promise all protection — will stay pursuit.   I will be there to take her
from your hands.

Don Luis.

I am somewhat old.

Sebastien.

Nay, sir, I hear your blood flows young and that you love these pastimes well—

Don Luis.

'T is true — assure your friend, the Duke, I 'll do his say. Commend me to him well— but here they come.

Sebastien.

See, that is she, Zerlina.

Don Luis.

How can I tell, where every one is masked?

Sebastien.

Pray, sir, and don yours too. It is an ancient custom that none shall show face till after the betrothal.

Don Luis.

A murrain on it. I 'd like to see the girl.

Sebastien.

Sir, 't is yonder maiden in the cloak.

Don Luis.

But there are two.

Sebastien.

Trust to the eye of love.

Don Luis.

Hey day! 't is blind. But this is your affair, not mine.

Sebastien.

I thank you, sir; I 'll wait you yonder in the copse.

[*They go up. Two masked figures approach.*

Donna Emilia.

[*Cloaked and masked.*

Sir, I implore forgiveness for my son. Think of his youth. I have come hither, unbeknown to my husband, to throw myself at your feet.

Don Alonzo.

Pray, madame, do not inconvenience yourself.

Donna Emilia.

Alonzo, you loved me once.

Don Alonzo.

Madame, we are too apt to be reminded at convenience of affections that are dead. You do not love

me now, and our interests conflict.   I 'll sacrifice no
morsel of my vengeance to a bran-stuffed memory.

Donna Emilia.

Alonzo, spare my child.

Don Alonzo.

Madame, I will kill him for dishonoring my house.

[Exit.

*[Don Luis enters.   Leporello points
to Donna Emilia.*

Don Luis.   *[Approaching.*

Fair Zerlina !

Donna Emilia.

[Aside, and masking quickly.

Don Luis here !

Don Luis.

Fair Zerlina, 't is needless to shade that face beneath
a mask; thy form betrays the beauty thou wouldst
hide; that graceful curve, those crisp, short curls upon
the neck betray thee but too well.   Thou art Zerlina.

Donna Emilia.   *[Aside.*

'T is long since he has wooed me.

Don Luis.

Pray have the dance with me. I am not young as you, nor fair, but there is a fire in my eye, and I have tilted in many a joust of love.

Donna Emilia. [*Aside.*

I do not doubt. Oh, sir!

Don Luis.

Give me thy hand. Come, dance with me to-night, and make thyself the proudest trophy I have won.

Donna Emilia. [*In a whisper.*

Sir, an you wish it. Oh, should my husband see me!

Don Luis.

Think not of him, of that decrepit dotard.

[*They go up.*

[*Dance. Don Juan and Zerlina come down.*

Don Juan.

Thou dancest like a fairy—the zephyr on the leaves, the wing of a gnat in the moonshine are not as light as thou.

Zerlina.

Fair sir, you—

12

Don Juan.

Nay, cease not, but take that ugly plaster from thy face that I may see thy lips.

Zerlina.

There —

Don Juan.

Now thou art good indeed, and may I kiss them? See, we are alone.

Zerlina.

I would not —

Don Juan.

When woman says she would not, she will, and when she will not, she would; therefore thou wouldst.

[*Kisses her.*

Zerlina.

Oh, sir, you steal my senses from me.

Don Juan.

Exchange is no robbery, and since thou hast stolen my heart —

Zerlina.

In so brief a space?

Don Juan.

Why should it take so long to light a fire? Thou hast kindled it and I am all aflame. And thou —

Zerlina.

I know not. Oh, this is some witchery; I am strangely moved. I know not myself. Sir, there was one other —

Don Juan.

Was! He is forgotten, as I forget all others now for you.

Zerlina.

Poor Sebastien!

[*Enter Sebastien* R. 2 E.

*Sebastien.**

Gently, sir, if you please; you are somewhat too officious.

Don Juan.

Who is this fellow?

Sebastien.

You must not kiss my wife that is to be.

Zerlina.

Let him alone, Sebastien.

---

* The brief scene which here follows is to be found in Molière's play of Don Juan.

Sebastien.

Not I. I will not. Because you are a gentleman, you come and caress our wives. Go and kiss your own.

Don Juan.

Never!

> [*Geralda comes down.*

Zerlina.

Oh, Sebastien, don't be angry. He's to marry me, and I will be a lady. You ought to be glad if you love me. You ought to be unselfish and rejoice.

Sebastien.

No, I would sooner see thee hanged.

> [*Sebastien and Zerlina engage in an animated discussion.*

Don Juan.

> [*Perceiving Geralda.*

Excuse me, you are very beautiful; do you belong to the village? What is your name?

Geralda.

Geralda, at your service. I am maid to a lady of high degree.

Don Juan.

What beauty! What piercing eyes!

Geralda.

Sir, you make me quite ashamed.

Don Juan.

Pray, tell me, pretty Geralda, are you married?

Geralda.

No, sir, but soon shall be.

Don Juan.

What! A beauty like you become the wife of some clodhopper! Nay, you deserve a better fate. I love you with all my heart. This passion is doubtless somewhat sudden, but it is owing to your great beauty. I love you as much in five minutes as I could another in six months. Let me take you from this wretched place, and place you in a position you deserve.

Geralda.

Sir, I do not know what to do when you speak. I do not know whether you speak the truth or not?

Don Juan.

What! you doubt my sincerity ?   Let me give you
one kiss as pledge.   [*Don Juan kisses Geralda.*

[*Zerlina breaks away from Sebastien.*

Zerlina.

Sir, what are you doing there with Geralda ?

Sebastien.

Zounds ! I will go and tell my influential friend to
help me.

[*Exit Sebastien.*

Don Juan.

I am telling her how much I admire you.

Geralda.

What does Zerlina want with you ?

Don Juan.

She is jealous because I speak to you, and wishes
me to marry her. [*Aside to Zerlina.*]   I will wager
she 'll tell you I was courting her.

Geralda.

Zerlina, it is needless for you to interfere; the gentleman has been won by my appearance and wishes to marry me.

Don Juan.   [*To Zerlina.*

What did I tell you? She 's a little foolish.

Zerlina.   [*To Geralda.*

Get ye hence! He would not look at you. This gentleman loves me, do you not, sir?

Don Juan.

[*Nods to Zerlina, then turns to Geralda.*

Did I not tell you so? Take no notice of her. The wine and the dance have excited her imagination. [*To Zerlina.*] All will be made known at the proper time when I claim you before all the world.

[*Walks to* L. *with Zerlina.*

Geralda.   [*Following them.*

Sir, put her in her place.

Zerlina.

Humble her now. Tell her that I am your choice.

Don Juan.

[*Taking their hands and glancing first at
one and then at the other.*

What necessity is there for me to speak? The one
who speaks the truth knows it, and there is no need
for me to tell it to her. Facts prove more than words,
and when I marry, you will see which of you two has
my heart. [*Aside to Geralda.*] Let her believe what
she will. [*Aside to Zerlina.*] Let her flatter herself.
I adore you only.*

Leporello.

[*Entering quickly.*

Sir, sir, the Don Alonzo comes. It is not safe here.

Lucia.

[*Entering quickly.*

Oh, sir, sir, there is some treachery afoot — come
hence!

Don Juan.

I am engaged now and will come anon.

Lucia.

Oh, Don Juan, there is a scheme abroad to kill you.

---

* The scene from Molière ends here.

Leporello.

Twelve men on horseback are in search of you.

Anna.   [*Coming down.*

Don Juan, you said you loved me.

·   *Don Juan.*   [*Embracing her.*

' Tis true, I adore you.

Lucia.

Don Juan, come — come with me.

Don Juan.

In a few minutes.

Leporello.

Fly, master !

Don Juan.

In a moment.

Geralda.

Oh, sir, do not forsake me !

Don Juan.   [*Embracing her.*

Never !

13

Zerlina.

I left Sebastien for you, and he loved me.

Don Juan.   [*Embracing her.*
Trust to me.

Anna.

Oh, sir, be true to me.

Don Juan.   [*Embracing her.*
I will.

Donna Emilia.

Don Luis, protect your son.

Don Juan.

My mother's voice!

Don Luis.

Horrible! I was nigh eloping with you. Don
Juan!   [*Enter Donna Elvira.*

Don Juan.

My father's voice!

Sebastien.   [*Coming down* L.

Now, sir, render me an account of your conduct.

Don Juan. [*Turning to him.*
With pleasure.

Donna Elvira.

[*Embracing Don Juan, on the other side.*
Come — come, dear Don Juan, come with thy
Elvira.

[*Don Juan turns, looks at Donna
Elvira, and exits.*

[CURTAIN.]

Act Three.

Act Three.

✠

[The oratory of the Duchess, in the cloister. Duchess and Lucia.

[Donna Julia, back of table, seated. Lucia seated right of table. Geralda brushing Donna Julia's hair.

Donna Julia.

Dear Lucia, I might have known your secret had the hours been calmer.

Lucia.

Madame, I live now but to serve you.

Donna Julia.

Nay, thou shalt not immolate thyself. With me all hope is dead. Chained to a horrible destiny, these gray walls will bring me all the happiness I 'll ever find. For thee, the world is thine, and Don Juan will love thee yet.

Lucia.

Nay, dear madame, I will stay with you. Don
Juan will never love poor me as I love him.

[*Enter Guzman, left door. Lucia rises.*

Guzman.

[*Bows to Donna Julia.*

Madame, the perfidy of Don Juan is but too sure;
he is unworthy, Lucia, of your love — madame, of
your regard. I bring the proofs of his guilt, which
you would not believe, — and you will now — pardon
me, madame — both be happier for that your love is
killed. He was about to carry away a girl of the village when Don Alonzo came upon the scene.

Donna Julia.

I will not believe, sir, that, in the face of all I — we
— dared for him, Don Juan would be guilty of such
treachery.

Lucia.

Alas, madame, I know him but too well.

Guzman. [*Guzman opens door.*

Enter.

[*Enter Zerlina and Sebastien.*

Guzman.

This maiden and this youth can tell the tale.

Donna Julia.

I do not care to hear it. I shall see him never more, and shall be happier for the tale untold.

Lucia.

And I, had I not seen it.

Donna Julia.

Thou ?

Lucia.

Poor child ! she was willing and unwilling.   'T was his art.

Donna Julia.

What is thy name ?

Zerlina.

Zerlina, an 't please your Highness.

Donna Julia.

And who is this ?

Zerlina.

Madame, he is my lover, an 't please your Grace.

14

Donna Julia.

Is this the man thou wert to marry ?

Sebastien.

Nay, your Grace, she was about to wed an old man and break my heart and disgrace herself.

Lucia.

Oh, hush ! you are too forward.

Donna Julia.

Nay, let it be — I am punished for my fault. [*To Zerlina.*] Child, thou art well saved. Wed not an old man. And Don Juan saved thee, did he not ?

Zerlina.

I know not, madame.

Donna Julia.

How ! Thou knowest not ?

Zerlina.

It seemed to me I knew not myself for a while. He said he loved me — then Sebastien came.

Donna Julia.

We need hear no more.   Guzman, let them go.

Sebastien.

Pray, your Grace, your protection, or I shall never wed Zerlina, since the old man —

Donna Julia.

See to it, Guzman, that they are married here. Have you means, sir, to support a wife ? — what are you ?

Sebastien.

An actor.

Lucia.

Madame, I have heard 't is no worse to wed an old man than to marry an actor.

Sebastien.

'T is true, madame, we are not generally liked.

Donna Julia.

What is thy line of art, man ?

Sebastien.

Madame, by your leave, I am a tragic actor.

Donna Julia.

Then I am sure you must need my purse.

Sebastien.

Madame, I never refuse a benefit.

[*Exeunt Zerlina, Sebastien, and Guzman.*

Donna Julia.

Those humble children will be happy.   How shall
we deal with Don Juan?

Lucia.

Forget him.

Donna Julia.

Assuredly.

Lucia.

It is certain we must never see him again.

Donna Julia.

Most certain.

Lucia.

Of course he will attempt to see us.

Donna Julia.

Of course.

Lucia.

And that must be prevented.

Donna Julia.

Certainly, but how ?

Lucia.

Ah, yes — how ?

Donna Julia.

We might send him a letter.

Lucia.

I am not strong in penmanship.

Donna Julia.

Nor I.

Lucia.

I do not think I could express myself with sufficient
force and determination in writing.

> [*A paper wrapped about a stone is thrown
> through window.*

Donna Julia and Lucia.   [*Starting.*

What is that ?

Geralda.

Madame, it looks like a piece of paper.

Donna Julia.

It caused too much noise for a piece of paper.

Geralda.

It is wrapped about a stone, madame.

Lucia

It may be a letter ?

Donna Julia.

A letter from whom ?   Who would dare to disturb our peace in this sanctuary ?

Lucia.

Perhaps —

Donna Julia.

You think —

Lucia.

It may be —

Donna Julia.

From —

Lucia.

Do not mention him.

Donna Julia.

No, never !

Lucia.

If it were from —

Donna Julia.

Him —

Lucia.

Of course we must not read it.

Donna Julia.

And if it is not?

Lucia.

Why, then, of course —

Donna Julia.

[*Looking fixedly at paper on floor.*

Let us not think of it.

Lucia.

[*With her eyes upon the paper.*

No, it will be better to turn our thoughts to other subjects.

Donna Julia.

Yes, that will be wiser.

Lucia.

We might, perhaps, first satisfy ourselves that it is not a letter.

Donna Julia.

And if it is —

Lucia.

Why, then we might make sure that it is not from him.

Donna Julia.

Of course, it could not be a missive for you.

Lucia. [*Rising.*

Pray, madame, why not?

Donna Julia.

Because, Don—he does not write letters to pages.

Lucia.

I forgot—then as I am quite sure it is not for me, there will be no harm—

Donna Julia.

It is thus I was thinking—

Lucia.

Geralda, pray bring me yon paper.

[*Geralda picks up paper; stone falls to floor. Holds up paper.*

Geralda.

Yes, madame, it is indeed a letter.

[*Goes back of Donna Julia.*

Lucia.

There is something written certainly, and in verse.

[*Reads.*

When Venus was flouted by Mars —

Was she, madame?

Donna Julia.

I do not recollect, but I have no doubt she was.

Lucia. [*Reads.*

When Venus was flouted by Mars,
The Goddess affirmed in a rage :
By the Sky, the Styx, and the Stars
She 'd follow the God as a page.

[*Stops suddenly.*

Oh!

Donna Julia. [*Laughs.*

Ha, ha, ha! for the life of me, dear Lucia, I cannot
refrain from laughing.

Lucia.

Madame, do you think this is intended for *me ?*

Donna Julia.

It seemeth so.

15

Lucia.

Oh, no, it cannot be; I should die of shame.

[*Reads.*

When Mars beheld love as a boy,
   Aware that the boy was the mother,
He vowed in excess of his joy—
   He could n't tell one from the other.

Donna Julia.

, I think there is no doubt; but read on, dear Lucia.

Lucia.   [*Reads.*

His ardor inflamed by the view
   Of adorable charms he had slighted,
He craved but a tryst to renew
   All the vows of affection he 'd plighted.

I 'll read no more. [*Scanning paper.*] There is no
more.

Donna Julia.

It is evident we must not be disturbed by a missive
such as yonder—

Lucia.

He is so persistent—

Donna Julia.

And *will* be the more we rebuff him. 'T is man's
nature.

Lucia.

Oh, madame, what are we to do?

Donna Julia.

I see but one way; we must send for him!

Lucia.

Yes! yes! no! no!

Donna Julia.

Hey day, Lucia, prithee be calm. I say we must send for him.

Lucia.

And then?

Donna Julia.

Throw ourselves upon his chivalry, point out to him that we are wedded to the church.

Lucia.

Yes, yes, we will send for him to see him again— to tell him we will never see him again.

Donna Julia.

What!

Lucia.

That we will never see him again.

Donna Julia.

Prithee, Geralda, look from the window; is there
any one watching?

> [*Geralda goes to window and looks out.*

Geralda.

Two figures by the cloister gate — the one is Don
Juan, the other his servant.

> [*Lucia goes to window and looks out.*

Lucia.

Ah!

Donna Julia.

How know you them, Geralda?

Geralda.

Madame — madame — I saw them in Sevilla.

Donna Julia.

Pray, Lucia, do not show yourself at the window.
What shall I write?

Lucia.   [*At table.*

Say, madame, *Dear Don Juan* — no, no — *Don
Juan* —

Donna Julia.   [*Writing.*

Don Juan —

Lucia.

Don Juan—Don Juan—madame, I can go no further than Don Juan.

Donna Julia.

I 'm well aware thou canst not.   There is no need
for many words.   *Don Juan, two poor women, who can
never see you more, will see you once again to bid you
farewell.   Enter by the cloister gate; a maid will lead
you to them.*   So—'t is well.   Geralda, cast it to him.
    [*A ladder is hooked on to the window.*

Geralda.

Oh !

Donna Julia.

What 's this ?

Lucia.

A ladder !

Donna Julia.

Wherefore ?

Geralda.

To climb up on.

Donna Julia.

Who ?

Geralda.

Don Juan.

Donna Julia.

To me!

Lucia.

To me!

Geralda.

To me!

[*Geralda fastens ladder, firmly.*

Geralda.

Pray, ladies, go, and I will say you 're far away.

Donna Julia.

Nay, in this sanctuary one may not lie. Go, dear
Lucia, with Geralda, and I will use some argument
and stern expostulation, and point out to him the
error of such audacious, infamous invasion.

Lucia.

Dear madame, I have known him long, and think
if you will both withdraw and let me speak with him,
I 'll make him go in peace.

Geralda.

Nay, nay, dear ladies, whilst I 'm alive to serve you
you shall not suffer insult. Pray go, and I will talk
to him with little choice of language.

Donna Julia.

My child, I appreciate such self-sacrifice, but I will not hear of it.

Lucia.

Nor I. He 's my cousin; I 've a right to chide him.

Donna Julia.

Perhaps [*Sigh*] it will be best that none should see him, but let us call the staid Ursula in, that she may bring him to a proper frame of mind.

Lucia.

Madame, is that your wish?

Donna Julia.

It is.

Lucia.

Then I must straight obey. Pray do you think the ladder safe?

Donna Julia.

No doubt. Come, we will send Ursula hither.

Lucia.

Come, Geralda.

Geralda.

I come, madame.

Donna Julia.

We 'll not go far.   [*Exeunt.*

Leporello.
         [*Head over window-sill.*

Rum tum tum.   There 's no one there.

Don Juan.   [*Appears.*

There 's no one here.

Leporello.

Where are they ?

Don Juan.

Donkey, thou hast hooked on to the wrong window.

Leporello.

Sir, 't was an error of judgment.   Hush, some one approaches.
       [*Enter Ursula, an aged housekeeper.*

Donna Julia.   [*Outside at door.*

You are to speak with him, and when he shows repentance, call me.

Lucia.

And me.

Geralda.

And me.

Ursula.

'T is many a year, madame, since I have spoken
with a man.

Donna Julia.

'T is for a noble purpose.

Ursula.

Madame, as you will.

Donna Julia.

Be seated in yon window.

> [*Ursula goes and sits in window.*

Leporello.

Rum tum tum.

> [*Ursula turns and sees him ; shrieks. Lepo-
> rello disappears. Donna Julia, Lucia,
> and Geralda enter at door.*

Donna Julia, Lucia, Geralda.

What is it ?

Ursula.

I 've seen the devil.

16

Donna Julia.

Nay, he's not as bad as that.

Lucia.

How dare you?

Geralda.

The devil indeed,— a very proper devil.

Ursula.

'T was a horrible sight.

Donna Julia.

I understand. Poor woman! 'T is so long since she has seen a man, he may seem strange to her.

Lucia.

Oh, yes, of course. Take courage, dear Ursula; you'll accustom yourself to the sight.

Geralda.

Yes, I did. They're not so bad.

Don Juan.

Pray, ladies, stay; I would converse awhile.

Donna Julia.

Lucia, Geralda, turn away and do not look at him. [*Over shoulder.*] Nay, we leave you to Ursula; she bears our message.

Ursula.

Was that his voice?

Lucia.

Aye, aye!

Ursula.

His voice is not as horrible as his face.

Lucia.

We 'll leave you now.

Ursula.

Oh, pray, stay —

Donna Julia.

Nay, nay, put off this foolish weakness. Speak to him. We go.

Don Juan.

Ladies, stay.   [*Disappears.*

[*Exeunt ladies.*

Leporello.   [*Appears.*

Rum tum tum.

Ursula.

Don Juan, I am commissioned — [*Turns and sees Leporello ; shrieks.*]   Oh! oh!

[*Leporello disappears.   Enter ladies.*

Donna Julia.

Again!   This is too foolish.

Ursula.

He is too hideous.   And I marvel much that you can bear to look on him.

Don Juan.   [*Appears.*

Dear Lucia — dear Julia, pray come speak with me.

Donna Julia.

Lucia, Geralda, turn away.   [*They turn.*

Ursula.

See, even you cannot bear to look on him.

Donna Julia.

But 't is for other cause.

Lucia.

And if we prove to you that we can eye him without fear —

Donna Julia.

Thou 'lt speak with him, wilt not, good Ursula?

Ursula.

I 'll try my very best, but 't is a fearful test.

Donna Julia.

'T is well.   Lucia, Geralda, turn.   [*They turn and face Don Juan.*]   We are now looking at him.

Ursula.

Aye, but you are all three trembling.

Don Juan.   [*After pause.*

Pray, say something.

Donna Julia.

We may not speak with you, Don Juan.

Lucia.

No, you must speak with Ursula.   I may not say a word to thee — think on 't, Don Juan — thou art so wicked I may not say a single word to thee, but Sister Ursula 's to speak with thee and thou with her, and if, Don Juan, thou showest repentance, then perchance I may — so now, I 'm not to say a word, and, dear Don

Juan, Don Juan — sir — I mean — you must not think
I care for thee a jot, no, not one jot any more, dear
Don Juan — Don Juan — sir, I mean — and I may
not say a word ; but, oh, Don Juan, do show repentance and I shall be so glad, altho' I do not care for
thee, because thou art so wicked. I must not speak
to thee at all —

[*She has been gradually approaching him.*

Don Juan.

I 'm really grieved at that, for I should like to hear
thy voice—if only for a moment.

Lucia.

Nay, dear Don Juan — Don Juan—sir, I mean.

Donna Julia.

Enough, Lucia. We must not stay an instant, nor
approach him, nor hold any converse with him. Ursula will explain how we do view his conduct, and that
his youth alone pleads his excuse, and therefore, on
that account, and if he shows repentance, *I* may forgive him.

Don Juan.

That 's truly kind of you.

Lucia.

I may perchance forgive him, if he shows repentance.

Don Juan.

Dear Lucia, come hither and let me whisper to thee how truly miserable I am.

Lucia.

Miserable !   [*Approaches.*

Don Juan.

Aye, wretched ! How well I know — but come nearer, 't is for thine ear alone.

Lucia.

Poor, dear Don Juan.   [*Approaching.*

Donna Julia.

Lucia, thou art mad ; come away.

Lucia.

But he is truly now repentant. 'T would be cruelty to deny him.

Don Juan.

Aye, dear Julia, 't would indeed. Come hither and I 'll explain.

Donna Julia.

Stay here, and I will go to him.

Lucia.

No, no, madame, you must not commit such folly.

Don Juan.

Geralda then may bring my message to you.

Geralda.

Aye — I am of no account, and I will go to him.

Donna Julia, Lucia.

Stay!

Ursula.

I think now I'm accustomed to his voice I may endure his face.

Donna Julia, Lucia, Geralda.

Ah!   [*Sigh.*

Donna Julia.

Ah! well, — 't is well — we go.   Pray, Don Juan, heed well the words of Ursula.   [*Sigh.*

[*Exeunt.*

Don Juan.

Come hither, dear Ursula.   [*Disappears.*

Ursula.

Pray, hide your face whilst I approach.   Little by little I may by glimpses accustom myself to the sight.

[*She sits in window.*

Don Juan.   [*Appears.*

Dear Ursula — I cannot see thy face, but I am sure that thou art beautiful.

Ursula.

His voice is very sweet.   I would his face were not so horrible.

Don Juan.

If thou couldst look upon me but with favor, how gladly would I gaze into thine eyes.

Ursula.

I have a message for thee, Don Juan.

Don Juan.

And I for thee !

Ursula.

From whom ?

Don Juan.

From Cupid.

17

Ursula.

I 've never heard of him.

Don Juan.

What! have those rebellious curls been ne'er caressed, those pouting lips had ne'er a kiss, and round about that taper waist has ne'er an arm —

[*Enter Donna Julia, Lucia, and Geralda.*

Donna Julia.

Don Juan, Don Alonzo comes; begone, and begone swiftly!

[*Don Juan disappears. Leporello appears, much frightened.*

Ursula.

[*Turns and perceives Leporello.*

Oh, horrible! another moment and I had kissed him.

Donna Julia, Lucia, Geralda.

What!

Ursula.

Peccavi — peccavi; let me hence.

Donna Julia.

Wicked Ursula, withdraw. I will come to thee anon.

Ursula.

Such winning ways with such a face! Peccavi!

[*Exit.*

[*Donna Julia, Lucia, and Geralda
go to window.*

Donna Julia.

Quickly begone, Don Juan and Leporello. Don Alonzo comes, nor does he come alone. To stay a moment now would be your death.

Don Juan.

I fear him not.

Donna Julia.

Well, then, consider my honor. For my sake, go.

Lucia.

Dear Don Juan, for my sake, go.

Don Juan.

Lucia, I 'll whisper one word in thine ear, and then I 'll go.

Lucia.

Well, then.   [*Don Juan kisses her.*

Don Juan.

I love thee only.

Lucia.

Thou sayest that to all.

Donna Julia.   [*At door.*

He comes. Begone!

Don Juan.

Nay, I fancy many. I love but one. 'T is thou!

Lucia.

Would I could believe thee.

Don Juan.

Believe me, 't is true. When may I see thee?

Donna Julia.

Quick — quick, begone!

Lucia.

I 'll — I 'll send thee a message.

Don Juan.

And I shall barely breathe till then.

Lucia.

Farewell.

Geralda. [*At door.*

He comes! he comes!

Don Juan.

Farewell.

Lucia.

Farewell.

Donna Julia.

Farewell. Cast loose the rope — throw the ladder down. Lucia, Geralda, leave me. I will face the Duke alone.

[*Exit Geralda.*

Lucia.

Nay, dear madame, let me stay. I cannot leave you now. [*Knocking at the door.*

Donna Julia.

Too late — 't is he. Would you had obeyed.

[*Knocking.*

Don Alonzo. [*Without.*

Open, madame.

[*Donna Julia unbars door. Enter Don Alonzo.*

Don Alonzo.

Madame, if I am well informed, Don Juan is here, or was here but a short while since.

Donna Julia.

He is not here.

Don Alonzo.

So I perceive.   But your lover has been here.

Donna Julia.

He is not my lover.

Don Alonzo.

I am pleased to hear it, madame.   I shall have the less difficulty in carrying out my purpose. [*Crosses to* R. *of Donna Julia.*]   Be pleased to take the pen you handle so deftly.

Donna Julia.

For what purpose ?

Don Alonzo.

To write to your lover.

Donna Julia.

I have told you he is not my lover.

Don Alonzo.

Very well then, to Don Juan.

Donna Julia.

It is to do him harm ?

Don Alonzo.

On the contrary, it is to put him out of harm's way.

Donna Julia.

What do you mean ?

Don Alonzo.

Write !

Lucia.

Madame, do not write.   I suspect —

Don Alonzo.

Who spoke ?   Who is this boy ?

Donna Julia.   [*Faintly.*

My — page.

Don Alonzo.

'T is well; he may then learn how to deal with a treacherous woman.

Donna Julia.

I am innocent.

Don Alonzo.

'T is a pleasure to hear you avow it.   Write !

Lucia.

Madame !

Don Alonzo.

Silence ! — write !

Donna Julia.

I am faint.   I cannot.

Lucia.

                    [*Crossing toward door.*

Madame ! Julia !

Don Alonzo.   [*Intercepts her.*

Ah, this is no boy.

Donna Julia.

It is Lucia — the bride of Don Juan — a witness to my innocence.

Don Alonzo. [*To Lucia.*

Donna Lucia, you shall have the pleasure of assisting — you must remain. [*Flinging her on one side.*

Lucia.

Coward!

Don Alonzo. [*Bowing.*

We have to bear the insults of your sex with humility.

[*Don Alonzo takes Donna Julia by wrist and forces her into chair. Lucia staggers back.*

Donna Julia.

Alonzo, you are crushing my wrist.

Don Alonzo.

Write!

Donna Julia.

You are torturing me. You are breaking my arm!

Don Alonzo.

Write!

Donna Julia.

I can bear no more.

18

Lucia.

Write! We will find some way to save him.

Don Alonzo.

Write!

Donna Julia.

What shall I say?   [*Fainting.*

Don Alonzo.

Ah — at last! [*Gives her pen.*] *Come at once.*

Lucia.

Coward! Coward! Coward!

Don Alonzo.

You do not write distinctly. *Come at once. The Duke has left the city.* Ah, that is well. *Lucia* — that is not clear — *Lucia is with me* — *the key I send herewith, it opens the postern* — *follow the winding stair* — *winding stair* — do you hear, madame? — *it leads to my door.*

Donna Julia.

I cannot, I will not.   [*Sinks fainting.*

Don Alonzo.

There is no need for more. It is enough — sign it.

Donna Julia.

I will not.

Don Alonzo.

No matter, he will know.   [*Takes paper.*

Lucia.

Julia! Julia! Listen!   [*Don Alonzo crosses to* L. C.

[*Don Juan, without, sings to the accompaniment of a guitar — the voice sounding through the open window at back — the moon has risen.*

Chill is the morning,
Sad is my heart,
Brief was the warning
That we must part: —
Fetters may bind thee,
O'er mountain and sea,
My love will find thee
Wherever thou be!

Chill is the morning,
Sad is my heart,
Brief was the warning
That we must part.
No one to guide me,
For love is my chart,
No one to call thee
But the voice of my heart.

Don Alonzo.

Your bird sings prettily, madame; we will put him in a cage for you.   *[Exit Don Alonzo.*

[Donna Julia and Lucia sit silent for a moment.

Lucia.   *[Springing up.*

The door. I can escape — maybe to warn him!

[As Lucia opens door, Geralda staggers in.

Geralda.   *[At door.*

Madame, madame, I have been hiding in the prayer-cell by the door — I could go no further — men are everywhere — it is impossible to pass.

Lucia.

Lost! Lost!

Donna Julia.

Lucia, see, see, I am broken-hearted. Curse me — it is my folly that has brought this upon thee.

Lucia.

Let us think only of him.

Donna Julia.

He will come.

Lucia.

And then we will find some way to save him.

Donna Julia.

Do you hear anything?

Lucia.

'T is a key turning in a lock.

Donna Julia.

The door creaks on its hinges.

Lucia.

'T is his hasty step on the stone stair.

Donna Julia.

All, all is lost.   Come hither — Lucia — let us pray
for him.

> [*Drags Lucia to oratory. Geralda remains
> in center of room.*

> [*Enter Don Juan. Donna Julia slips back
> and bolts door, stands back to door.*

Don Juan.

At last! What perils beset the road of love. But
't were not worth the winning were it easy, Lucia —
no, Julia — no, 't is not Lucia — it is Julia — no, 't is
not Julia — 't is Geralda — by the powers, a fair sub-
stitute — and since thy mistress tarries, I 'll mark each

moment to her cost with a kiss, and since two tarry, two kisses are but fair. Come, Geralda—for the prettiest maid I ken, thou hast the solemnest face. Zounds! I would wager by thy face thou hast made up thy mind to bury thy love, and I 've a duty to disinter it. [*His arms about her waist.*] There, I could resurrect the veriest, profoundest corpse of love with such a kiss!

[*Geralda sinks on her knees and weeps.*

Don Juan.

Pray, is that for joy or for sorrow? 'T is the first time kiss of mine caused such effect.

Geralda.

Oh, sir, fly —you are lost!

Don Juan.

Is it not a little wearying that every woman I meet says, Fly; and every maiden I kiss cries, Lost!

Geralda.

Sir, you are beset!

Don Juan.

In truth I am, with a sin.

Geralda.

There are "*men*" everywhere.

Don Juan.

More is the pity—would there were naught but "*maidens.*"

Geralda.

Sir, you are betrayed!

Don Juan.

Every man is that once or more times.

Geralda.

Is there nothing will open your eyes to your danger?

Don Juan.

My danger lies before me, and I confess myself already conquered. Love without danger is meat without sauce. Whom dost thou fear, pretty one,— the Donna Julia?

Donna Julia.

[*Going toward Don Juan.*

Don Juan, fly whilst there is yet time!

Don Juan.

And here 's another one.

Donna Julia.

Don Juan, thou art lost — betrayed.   And I — I have betrayed thee.

Don Juan.

Nay, sweet Julia, 't was not a moment since this tiny message was slipt into my hands, and have I not come swiftly ?

Donna Julia.

Aye, aye, all too swift — ere I could find means to warn thee.   Thou art lost !

Don Juan.

Are not these words by thy hand ?

Donna Julia.

It is my hand that kills thee.   Would I had died before I wrote them.

Don Juan.

I do not understand.

Donna Julia.

Listen — dost hear the clash of steel, the tramp of men ?

Don Juan.

Nay, I hear naught.

Donna Julia.

Still, they are there — there by the door, watching to kill thee.

Don Juan.

Thou ravest, Julia. No one is there. I passed up the stair as free as air.

Donna Julia.

Oh, yes! oh, yes!

Don Juan.

Had an enemy lurked in the shadow, he would have killed me then.

Donna Julia.

Aye, aye, the trap was set, the passage free and no way out. [*Pointing at door.*] Don Alonzo is there.

Don Juan.

Nay, Julia, by thy note of hand, he 's left the town.

Donna Julia.

I lied — he 's there.

Don Juan.

He 's there!
19

Donna Julia.

Oh, would I had died — would he had killed me — see my wrist — he forced me — with his iron hand — he crushed the bone; in torture — in torture, Don Juan, I wrote the lines that bring thee here.

Don Juan.

My poor Julia — how is thy tiny wrist bruised ?

Donna Julia.

Oh, think not of me — pity me not — curse me rather that I have brought you to this. Oh, is there no way out?

Don Juan.

Nay, nay, why should I curse thee, Julia ?

Donna Julia.

Aye, curse me; an' had I loved thee I would not have written this — he had killed me rather.

Don Juan.

What, dost thou not love me ?

Donna Julia.

Oh, Don Juan, know that death has no terrors to a woman who protects her love.

Don Juan.

This is strange news. I thought all women loved
me. I think Lucia would have died.

Donna Julia.

Aye, aye, she loves thee truly.

Lucia. [*Coming from recess.*

You are wasting precious time in idle words.

Don Juan.

Lucia !

Lucia.

Don Juan !

Don Juan.

There is an ancient saw which saith, *Absence makes
the heart grow fonder*, and I have missed thee every
minute since we parted.

Lucia.

Don Juan !

Don Juan.

Mine eyes must bear to thine a thousand messages
of love, and ne'er was dove's flight swift as answering
glance of thine. Lucia, when we go hence, we 'll ne'er
be parted more.

Lucia.

Alas, alas ! how will you safely hence ?

Don Juan.

Thou too ?   And is it true that there is so much
peril ?

Lucia.

The Duke has trapped you here to kill you.

Don Juan.

It dawns upon me, I am in danger.   He does not
wish to fight me fair, and would rather play assassin
here ?

Lucia.

Aye, aye, aye, aye, 't is so !
     [*Lucia goes to window ; Donna Julia follows.*

Don Juan.

There 's some way out of everything.   Perchance,
the window.   [*Going to window.*]   Let me reflect.
Thou sayest Don Alonzo 's there — no other door ?
This window is too high..   How many men ?

Geralda.

Sir, more than a score.

Don Juan.

They are too many. [*Lays aside his cloak and hat.*] It seems that I 'm to die. I 'm somewhat young, and I had thought of many years of pleasure. Death ! It is not beautiful, and I 've no longing for any other world but this. It doth seem strange that I should die so soon.

Donna Julia.

Would he had cut off the hand before I held the pen.

Don Juan.

I 've heard a wicked pen can wreck a many lives. Why should I stand inactive here ? There may be hope. Perchance this Duke hath still some valor in his veins. Do you withdraw, and I will challenge him to single combat, or two or three — twenty to one is mere assassination.

Donna Julia.

Vain hope, the trap is too well set — why, will he argue, should he risk his life ?

Don Juan.

Nay, I will try. [*Goes to door.*] Hey, Don Alonzo — you without — come in ! Bring one — bring two — I 'll fight you three to one, and if I win I 'm free.

[*Beats on door with his hands.*]   Hear me, without,
come in — bring four.   Alonzo, Duke of Navarro, dost
hear?   Coward, dost thou hear?   Come in and meet
me like a man.   Assassin, enter.   I am here.— I have
insulted him in many various ways.   There is no
sound — they are not there — I 'll open.

Donna Julia and Lucia.

[*Holding him back.*

No!   No!

Don Alonzo.   [*Without.*

Open!

Don Juan.

At last.   Hast heard me, sir?   Wilt fight me?   I
am ready here.

Don Alonzo.

Open, and you will know.

Don Juan.

How many are you?

Don Alonzo.

Enough to kill you.

Don Juan.

Wilt fight me three to one, and if I conquer, am I
free?

Don Alonzo.

> [*Battering at door renewed.*

Open! This is no duel of honorable men —'t is the execution of a criminal. You, Don Juan, are the condemned. Open!

Don Juan.

Coward! Thus do assassins e'er excuse their crimes.

> [*A rope ladder is thrown through window.*

Lucia.

Look! look! the ladder — thou art saved, saved, Don Juan!

> [*They go to window. Knocking is renewed.*

Donna Julia.

Swiftly—swiftly—adjust the steps—the door is strong.

Lucia.

See, 't was Leporello by yonder buttress threw the rope. Ah!

Don Juan.

In vain, see where they stand — some dozen men — the trap is well set.

Lucia.

Don Juan, I can save thee! Give me thy cloak and hat—here is a sword; they will not know me in the darkness. Hide yonder 'neath the altar—I will go for thee.

Don Juan.

Silence, Lucia, wouldst thou dub me coward?

Lucia.

What is my life to thine—and who will miss me?

Don Juan.

I, if I live.

Lucia.

Nay, let me go and thou art saved.

Don Juan.

Not, an' if I have to bind thee.

Lucia.

Don Juan, dear Don Juan—oh, let me go. Lived I one hundred years from now, there 'd be no moment in it sweet as death for thee, and in that death no suffering as life without thee.

Don Juan.

Nay, love, it may not be—here I 'll await them.
'T is nothing, death — only unman me not, and when
I fight cheer me, yet say no word of sorrow or of pain.

Lucia.

I 'll fight then by thy side.

Don Juan.

That must thou not.   I think I 'd hate thee if I
saw thee fight.

Lucia.

Hate me !   Go, sword !

     [*Throws sword down.   Hammering without
        at door.*

Donna Julia.

Don Juan—the door—I can no longer hold.

Don Juan.

What sayest thou, Julia, shall I open and let them
enter one by one ?

Donna Julia.

Thou couldst not; they would surely break their
way.

20

Lucia.
> [*Seizing cloak and hat.*

I'll save him now whether he will or no. [*Takes sword.*
> [*Knocking at door.*

Don Juan.

The door gives way. Fly to your prayers, thou and Lucia! and let *me* fight.

Lucia.
> [*Going through window.*

Farewell, Don Juan, farewell.
> [*Guzman appears through panel in wall.*

Guzman.

Don Juan.

Don Juan.

Who speaks?

Guzman.

Don Juan, I am in time.   Here is thy way.

Donna Julia.

Ah! saved, saved, Guzman — thank heaven!
> [*Voices and clash of steel outside window.*

Don Juan.

Aye, saved!

Guzman.

Come.

Don Juan.

Lucia, dear Lucia, come.

Guzman.

Whose voice is that — where is Lucia?

Don Juan.

What!

Donna Julia.

Ah, heaven! [*Looking through window and pointing.*] There, there is Lucia.

Don Juan.

There! Alas, too late.

Guzman.

Come.   [*Loud knocking at door.*

Guzman.

You cannot save her. Come.

Don Juan.

Come, I? I go in safety, whilst she dies for me? Nay, I will die with her or for her as she would die for me. Lucia, I come — I come! [*Exit through window.*

[*Door falls in. Enter Don Alonzo. Men stand in door. Donna Julia stands fainting, dazed.*

Don Alonzo.

Ah! Escaped — Guzman, *you* have connived.

[*Clash of steel. Voices.*

Don Alonzo.

Ah!

Donna Julia.

Heaven save them!

Don Alonzo.

Listen, madame! [*Holds her by wrist.*

[*Clash of steel. Silence.*

Don Alonzo.

Come, madame, I will show you your lover. [*Drags her to window. Looking out; light of torches outside.*] Hold the torch to his face. Who is that?

A voice.

It is the page.

Don Alonzo.

And there?

A voice.

Don Juan —

Don Alonzo.

Dead?

A voice.

Wounded.

Don Alonzo.

Gag him with that!   [*Throws glove out of window.*
                           [*Donna Julia faints.*

[CURTAIN.]

Act Four.

Act Four.

✠

A DUNGEON.

[*Don Juan and Lucia discovered lying in separate corners.   Table by fire; Leporello, Zerlina, and Sebastien.*

Sebastien.

'T is most fortunate they fell to our charge.

Zerlina.

Poor youth !   He 's comely enough, I trow, to have deserved a better fate.

Sebastien.

I warrant the Duke will torture him.

Zerlina.

In his delirium he spoke of naught but Lucia. [*Crossing over and looking at Don Juan.*]   He sleeps now calmly — he mends rapidly.   Poor lad !

21

Leporello.

He had much better died.

Sebastien.

True, he will recover to a worse disease.

Leporello.

[*Rising — looking at Lucia.*

She sleeps also. How she did nurse and watch him, and never closed an eye. Poor creatures! But tell me, pray, how came you here a jailer?

Sebastien.

Ah, sir, 't is a long story and a short story. It happened in a little while, but takes a long while telling. 'T is a case of revenge.

Leporello.

Ah, sir, I have a surfeit of horrors — make it brief.

Sebastien.

Then, sir, know I 'm an actor.

Leporello.

Sir, I said I had a surfeit of horrors.

Sebastien.

Recently, sir, I appeared in Saragossa in a play of value — a play of consistency — a play, sir, of action — a play of pungent satire — a play, sir, which fired at bribery, theft, peculation, robbery, gambling, and wholesale fraud; sir, I was hissed and pelted. I left the stage, sir, and for revenge became a jailer.

Leporello.

I do not take you, sir?

Sebastien.

Sir, sooner or later they will all come here, and then I can e'en force them to listen to me.

Leporello.

Oh, horrible! heaven help them, poor wretches! You will not practise such cruelty on Don Juan?

Sebastien.

Nay, I have naught but affection for him.

Leporello.

I too, yet he has treated me ill. My tale of devotion would cause your tears to flow; no words express

his ingratitude.   I warned and counseled him at all
time, and had he listened to my teachings he had not
now been here.

Zerlina.

Wise sir, can you do naught to save him ?

Leporello.

Madame, I have indeed cogitated on a plan of much
excellence, but it will need your aid.

Zerlina.

Sir, you may count on me.

Leporello.

On you too, sir ?

Sebastien.

Pray, sir, command me.

Leporello.

Then it is this.   Your handsome wife shall take the
place of Donna Lucia, whilst you impersonate the Don
Juan.   You give the password, and myself will lead
the Don Juan from here.

Sebastien.

Is there no danger attending such a scheme ?

Leporello.

Surely, sir. The Duke will no doubt hang you.

Sebastien.

Sir, 't is a beautiful thought, a deed of noble heroism. Willingly I 'd sacrifice myself for yonder youth.

Leporello.

Noble being !

Sebastien.

If 't could be done without danger to myself.

Zerlina.

I too would gladly run the risk were there no danger.

Leporello.

You are both of nature's noblest mold.

Zerlina.

Oh, sir, you flatter us. We need no thanks ; we do our humblest best.

Leporello.

Another plan to free poor Don Juan is in my mind matured.

Sebastien.

You have a vast intellect, sir.

Leporello.

Enough for two. With your connivance I 'll take the place of Don Juan.

Zerlina.

Ah, noble man!

Leporello.

I never had a petty thought. You shall conduct him hence and vow he 's Leporello, and *I* will suffer death.

Zerlina and Sebastien.   [*Both rise.*

Sir! sir!

Sebastien.

Sir, you will be made a saint.

Leporello.

That is my sole ambition; be sure to take a plaster of my face when I am dead. I would not have them spoil my features in my statues.

Sebastien.

Trust, sir, to us.

Leporello.

Some saints are made so ugly.

Sebastien.

That shall not be the case with you. Will you
occupy his place, sir, now, at once, before they come
the rounds?

Leporello.

No, I will consider of the matter.

[*Exit Leporello.*

Sebastien.

Saintly man! Oh, what devotion! Let us hence
to our midday meal, Zerlina, the whilst the prisoners
sleep.   [*Exeunt.*

Don Juan.   [*Sings.*

Chill is the morning,
Sad is my heart.

[*Waking.*] What strange place is this?—what horrid bed? I thought I lay on down and kisses came
upon my brow. [*Lifting himself up.*] Lucia!

Lucia.

Who spoke?

Don Juan.

Lucia!

Lucia.

Don Juan, is 't thou ?

Don Juan.

Lucia, what is this ? — where am I ?

Lucia.

Hush, sleep! thou hast been ill.

Don Juan.

Ill! aye, my temples throb; I would hence — I
would come to thee.

Lucia.

Lie still! lie still !

Don Juan.

  [*Drags himself off couch to end of his chain.*
Lucia, I cannot *come* to thee.

Lucia.

Lie still, dear Don Juan! I come to thee.
  [*Lucia crosses over and sits on foot of pallet.*

Don Juan.

Lucia, thou art well ?

Lucia.

Aye; I am well.

Don Juan.

This is a gloomy place, and I am all an ache. Why are we here?

Lucia.

Oh, Don Juan, it was for loving Donna Julia.

Don Juan.

I do remember something of it, but I did never love the Donna Julia.

Lucia.

Then for the pretense.

Don Juan.

This seems large punishment for an hour's entertainment.

Lucia.

Dear Don Juan, thou wert a poacher.

Don Juan.

Nay, 't was all a frolic. I do remember hearing of a youth jailed six moons for the kissing of a lass. I 'd wish to see that girl.

22

Lucia.

Why, Don Juan?

Don Juan.

One kiss, six months! She must be very beautiful.

Lucia.

Hush! thy mind wanders.

Don Juan.

Nay, I have had one long, continuous dream of *thee*, Lucia. Give me thy hand. Have I brought thee to this?

Lucia.

Nay, 't was of my own choosing.

Don Juan.

Devotion bound to folly, buried in one grave; but I remember now thou fought'st for me. Thou couldst not save me; I could not save thee. I fell, and thou, Lucia, thou art wounded?

Lucia.

Nay, a woman's weakness proved my strength. I swooned, and then they thought me dead.

Don Juan.

Heaven be praised! And now thou must go free. Surely the Don Alonzo will not punish *thee*?

Lucia.

I am happier here than I could elsewhere be without thee.

Don Juan.

Lucia, I am a weather-vane to love. If comes the south wind, laden with the perfume of flowers, I do point that way, and when the north wind blows, straight from the rainbow-icebergs, and the crisp green seas, quick I turn to that. I am for the north, the south, the east, and the west. Hot passion consumes me, cold love spurs me, haughty love rouses me, and a purring love soothes me. I am not worthy of thee.

Lucia.

Hush, I have not thought of that. I love thee.

Don Juan.

Let me look into thine eyes, Lucia; I see all there. Thou art cold, thou art on fire, thou art proud and thou art gentle. Thou 'lt be this one day and that another, and thus the weather-vane will ever point with thee. I love thee and thou wilt hold me ever. All on earth is beautiful by contrast. Would all women knew it, and trusted not the dull monotony of estimable, exacting love.

Lucia.

Be still, dear Don Juan; thy mind 's astray.

Don Juan.

Whenever a man proclaims a truth, he 's mad. Lucia, when we go hence we 'll leave the world and live alone. Thou with me. I see a red-roofed cottage nestling in the trees and flowers by the porch. And thou and I stand there; the sun is setting, and the rooks fly homeward. Love; love and peace.

Lucia.

Don Juan! Don Juan!

Don Juan. [*Sings.*

Love had a fancy to rest,
Far from the world and its jest;
Love had a fancy to rest,
Love with itself on its breast.

Lucia.

Don Juan! Don Juan!

Don Juan.

Lucia, Lucia, I love thee, and I will cleave to thee through happiness and sorrow, through youth and age, from here unto the grave; in word and thought, in wish and deed, I will be true to thee, to thee, Lucia. Ah! Seal me the compact with a kiss.

[*Lucia leans over; their lips meet.*

Lucia.

Freely! gladly! I give it, Don Juan; thine, thine!

Don Juan. [*Sinks back.*

Saved, saved, Lucia! Ah!

[*The door opens. Enter Sebastien ushering in Donna Emilia and Don Luis. Lucia rises.*

Sebastien.

I do it at my peril, since the orders are that no one should see the prisoners.

[*Don Luis gives him money.*

Donna Emilia.

Sir, I trust my poor son is well cared for?

Sebastien.

Madame, he has every comfort that my means afford.

Don Luis.

This does not smack of luxury.

Sebastien.

Sir, I can do better with a better purse.

Don Luis.   [*Giving money.*

There, sir, supply him with food and bedding and change this dungeon for a better.

Sebastien.

My Lord, I can give him healthy quarters and three meals a day.

Don Luis.

See to it.

Sebastien.

Sir, I leave you for five minutes.

Don Luis.

It is well.   [*Exit Sebastien.*

Don Luis. [*Coming down steps.*

Ah, Don Juan, my son, with all my care, with all my rigorous discipline, and what has brought thee now to this?

Don Juan. [*Listlessly.*

An had you taught me more, I should have less inquired. Had you less forbidden, I should have less desired. An had you less temptation shown, I should have less temptations known.

Donna Emilia. [*In door.*

That girl has wrought his ruin.

Lucia.

'Fore heaven, madame, an thou knowest that is false. I care for him because I love him, and those who should have cared for him do care naught for him. We are betrothed, and heaven please to free us from this cell, we 'll wed.

Donna Emilia.

[*Coming down steps.*

'T is false, and thou shalt never wed him. We come with message from the Duke, who in his mercy doth afford a pardon. We have far higher aims than dowerless and nameless girl. Don Juan, thou mayst go free.

Don Juan.

Ah!

Don Luis.

If thou wilt wed — high honor too it is — the Donna Elvira, sister to the Duke.

Donna Emilia.

And she is here, herself, to tell you of this boon and how she plagued the Duke to grant her this concession. [*Enter Donna Elvira.*

Donna Elvira.

[*Running down steps.*

Ah, Don Juan, thou naughty, naughty boy — thou hast enough endured, I trow, and dost repent thee of thy fault? I come and bring thee freedom, love, wealth, happiness, and joy. The Duke consents that we should wed. Come now, those shackles fall, and none you'll know but mine.

Don Juan.

I would be glad of freedom.

Don Luis.

Wed the Donna Elvira, and 't is yours.

Don Juan.

An if I will not?

Don Luis.

Then, alas! the Duke is adamant—you die.

Don Juan.

[*Twining his arms about Lucia.*

Then I would rather die.

Donna Elvira.

Oh, for such scorn he doth deserve a thousand deaths.

Donna Emilia.

Don Juan, Don Juan, my son, reflect.

[*Enter jailer.*

Sebastien.

Madame, the time allowed is past; you must now all depart.

Don Luis.

Alas, alas, my son, would you bring my gray hairs with sorrow to the grave?

Don Juan.

Sir, an my curls were never tinged with sin.

Donna Emilia.

Oh, Don Juan, consent to wed this lady or you die.

23

Lucia.

Think not of me, Don Juan, I bid you go and save your life. Go, and for my sake go and make me happy in the knowledge that you live.

Don Juan.   [*Sings.*

Love had a fancy to rest,
Far from the world and its jest;
Love had a fancy to rest,
Love with itself on its breast.

Lucia, give me thy hand. Come, bring some sword and hack these hands in two—'t is only thus that you may part us.

Sebastien.

I pray you, sir and good ladies both, you must depart.

Donna Emilia.

Alas, alas! we go.   [*Exit weeping.*

Don Luis.

My son, my son, reflect. Think on this, think on this, and when his highness comes, tell him you 're molded to his will. Farewell, I hope to hear good news of you.

Don Juan.

Farewell, my father—I owe thee some three days of pleasure. [*Exit Don Luis.*

Donna Elvira.

Don Juan, there is no venom like a woman's hate, and thou shalt taste the poison soon. Thou scornst me and for her—thou shalt have cause in torture soon to curse thy pretty love. Farewell to thee, farewell, thou bride of Don Juan. [*Exit Donna Elvira.*

Lucia.

Oh, Don Juan, is all hope gone?

Don Juan.

With thee by my side I am content.
[*Enter Leporello.*

Leporello.

Sir, sir, are you conscious?

Don Juan.

I am aware of some things.

Leporello.

I have conceived a mighty scheme to save you both.

Don Juan.

What is it ?

[*Enter Gvzman and Sebastien.*

Guzman.

Silence, fool ! Sebastien, stand on guard. Don Juan, thy folly has brought thee to a sorry pass — yet for my love for thee and thee, Lucia, I cannot see you perish both, e'en tho' I break my duty to the Inquisition. Here are two noble souls prepared to take your place.

[*Enter Donna Julia and Geralda, cloaked.*

Guzman.

Sebastien, the key !

Don Juan.

Do they incur no danger ?

Guzman.

None.

Don Juan.

Who are they ?

Donna Julia.

I brought you here — I 'll see you hence.

Don Juan.

Ah, Donna Julia!

    Lucia.   [*Going to her.*

Donna Julia!

    Donna Julia.

Swiftly, dear Lucia, take this cloak.

    Guzman.

Unlock the chain and let Geralda take his place, the Duke Alonzo comes.

    Leporello.

Sir! sir! I hear the Don Alonzo's step.

    Guzman.

Too late! Too late!

    Sebastien.

I am lost! Lost!

    Guzman.

Nay, swiftly, Sebastien, free Don Juan —

      [*Sebastien unlocks chain.*

Don Juan.

I am too weak to stand.

[*Geralda takes Don Juan's place.*

Guzman.

Don Juan, thou *must* stand, and stand firm.   Stand
for thy freedom — stand firm for Lucia's sake.

Don Juan.

Give me a sword.

Guzman.

Geralda, hand him the sword.

Don Juan.

What must I do?

Guzman.

Withdraw with Lucia in yon shadow.   Alonzo will
enter and address the Donna Julia and Geralda, thinking they are you.   He'll lay his sword upon the
board to sign your warrant — then seize it swiftly,
thou Lucia, and, at the point of both your sword and
his, make good your safety.   Hush! Don Alonzo
comes.

Leporello.

Master, be firm, remember all the fence I taught you.

> [*Exit Leporello, Guzman, Sebastien. Donna Julia sits on pallet ; Geralda lies on same. Lights are low. Red light.*

Don Juan. [*Sings.*

When Venus was flouted by Mars,
The goddess —

Lucia.

Oh, hush! Don Juan, dear Don Juan, you know now what you are to do.

Don Juan.

Aye, aye, I am to protect you, am I not?

Lucia.

Aye, but yourself the more. We are to go in safety. Only be firm, and then we shall be away from here and happy.

Don Juan.

Happy, happy, happy!

Lucia.

[*Dragging Don Juan into shadow at back.*

Don Juan, he comes! he comes!

Don Juan.

Who comes?

Lucia.

Don Alonzo.

Donna Julia.

Don Juan, be firm. Silence, he comes!

[*Enter Don Alonzo.*

Don Alonzo.

'T is a pity the Donna Julia is not here to see you thus. Sir, you have now discovered what it is to insult my house. Hie, man —

[*Enter Sebastien.*

Don Alonzo.   [*To Donna Julia.*

I see you have the wisdom to be silent. Words will avail thee naught, 't is true. Go tell Don Pizarro that I sign the warrant — prepare the guards!

[*Don Alonzo sits at table. Exit Sebastien.*

Don Juan.

Let me get *at* him.

Don Alonzo.

Who spoke ?

Geralda.

I, sir, the Donna Lucia.

Don Alonzo.

Ah, you are here too.   Such devotion surely needs
'some recompense, and you shall have it.

> [*Lays sword on table and prepares to write.
> Lucia creeps up.*

Don Alonzo.

I can write better with the sword than with a pen —
still, this pen, hear you, is now drawing some quantity
of blood.

Lucia　　　　[*Taking sword.*

Aye, sir, and this sword too, unless we both go free.

Don Alonzo.

> [*Springs up and faces about.*

What !
24

Don Juan.

[*Faces him, sword in hand.*

Ah, Don Alonzo, murderer — coward! I have a mind to kill thee.

Don Alonzo.

Betrayed!

Don Juan.

Avenged!

Donna Julia   [*Rising.*

Avenged, Don Alonzo! Thought you whilst I had life in me I 'd see this poor youth sacrificed to your senseless anger, and I the cause of his suffering?

Don Alonzo.

Oh, for a weapon!

Don Juan.

Now change your warrant — 't is, I doubt not, for our deaths — to one for freedom, and perforce perform your only virtuous act. Write!

Don Alonzo.

Hie! Hie! without!

Don Juan.

Utter one other sound and I will run thee through.
Act swiftly. Write!   [*Don Juan's sword closer.*

Don Alonzo.

What shall I write?

Don Juan.

I will cleave to thee through happiness and sorrow
— through youth —

Lucia.

No! No! Don Juan — recollect thyself.

Don Alonzo.

Ah! Down with that sword!

Don Juan.   [*Lunging at him.*

Thro' with that sword.

Don Alonzo.

A madman!

Don Juan.

Write! Lucia, Lucia, what shall he write? — be
quick, I can barely stand.

Lucia.

Pass free Donna Lucia, Julia, Geralda, Don Juan.

Don Alonzo.

May the devil bear me away —

Don Juan.

He will.   First write — or —

> [*Threatens with sword.*
> [*Don Alonzo writes.*

Don Juan.

Give me the paper.

Donna Julia.

How are the tables turned!

Don Alonzo.

Yes, madame, for a while — but for a little while only.

Lucia.

Madame, you go with us — quick —

Don Juan.

Quick.   [*Handing her paper.   To Lucia, aside.*]

Quick — quickly go — Donna Julia, go — Geralda — Lucia — Ah! — go! go! quickly, swiftly. I can barely stand. [*They pass behind him.*

Don Alonzo.

Ah!

Don Juan.

Off! Off!

Lucia.

Let me stay by your side.

Don Juan.

Go! — until I hear your footsteps some fifty paces, I do not pass the door, nor close it — call to me from thence.

[*Don Alonzo advances toward Don Juan, who keeps him feebly off.*

Don Juan.

Go, Lucia, go!

Lucia. [*Passing out of door.*

My mind misgives me.

[*Leporello at grating.*

Leporello.

Master, master, the guards are coming!

Don Alonzo.

Now, madman!

Don Juan.

Lucia, where are you?

Lucia.   [*From a distance.*

Safe — safe, Don Juan, come — come!

Don Juan.

I come, Lucia. [*Staggers to door. Holding on to door.*] I cannot go around it. Lucia — Lucia —oh, if there were in me but one more drop of blood! Fly, Lucia! *   [*Sword falls from his hand. Staggers.*

Don Alonzo.

Ah, at last. Hie — hie — without, to the rescue!

[*Springs at sword.*

Don Juan.   [*Stands singing.*

       Chill is the morning,
       Sad is my heart.   [*Gradually falls on his knees.*] Lucia — Lucia —

     [*Enter Lucia. Don Juan falls. Lucia kneels by his side.*

* See note on page 191.

Don Juan.

Love had a fancy to rest,
Alone with itself on its breast.   [*Sinks down.*

[*Don Alonzo takes sword to strike.*
Enter Guzman.

Guzman.

Stay — here intervenes a higher power, Death !

Lucia.

[*Raising her arms, kneeling by body.*

And love ! love !

[CURTAIN.]

From this point the comedy has been recently changed in order to satisfy those who prefer an agreeable ending. Don Juan is made to fight his way to the stone steps which lead to the door of the dungeon. He laughs wildly and lunges fiercely at Don Alonzo, who endeavors to intercept him. Having reached the stone steps, he discovers that he is too feeble to climb them with his face to the foe. He sinks upon his knees, and, still with his sword warding off Don Alonzo, commences to drag himself up, but is about to succumb when Lucia appears, and with her assistance the heavy door is finally swung to in the very face of the enraged Duke. As the curtain descends the wild laughter of Don Juan is still heard, whilst the face of Leporello appears at the grating.